THE EMPTY WORLD

4

THE LOST PORTAL

DAVID K. ANDERSON

THE EMPTY WORLD

BOOK 4

THE LOST
PORTAL

DAVID K. ANDERSON

Magical Scrivener Press
22 Hawkstead Hollow
Nashua, NH 03063

www.magicalscrivener.com

Publisher's Note: This is a work of fiction. Names, characters, places, and incidents are a product of the author's imagination. Locales and public names are sometimes used for atmospheric purposes. Any resemblance to actual people, living or dead, or to businesses, companies, events, institutions, or locales is completely coincidental.

Ordering Information: Special discounts are available on quantity purchases by corporations, associations, and others. For details, contact the publisher at the address above.

David K. Anderson – First Edition

ISBN 978-1-939233-92-9

Printed in the United States of America

Dedication: For my three brothers, Dick, Dennis and Tim, and for Gary King, Jay Savage, Allan Satrape, Karen Swanson, Jane Onges, Pat Flaherty, and Sue Quagge.

It is because of these wonderful people, while growing into young adulthood, that I have been inspired to write about that age group and about relationships among family and friends.

CHAPTER 1

"**I** have to stay and help find Cory. It's just as much my fault he's here as it is his," Christy Walker argued, looking directly at her dad.

The rest of the group—Detective Lockhart; Christy's grandfather, Jack; and her best friend, Trevor— were all hanging back to let father and daughter talk it out. The five of them were in an underground city, in an immense room they'd discovered while trying to collect Cory and return to earth. But when they'd arrived, they found a goodbye note explaining his plan to use a portal to another city, where he hoped there was a cure for his paralysis.

"No, Christy, you're going home as soon as we decide on a rescue plan."

Doug Walker looked around at the others for support but Jack, Detective Lockhart and Trevor kept their eyes on the floor, none of them wanting to meet Doug's gaze. The silence went on for half a minute before Jack cleared his throat and spoke.

"I think Christy will not only be a big help, but I think she's essential for us to succeed in finding Cory. Nobody knows this world like she does, with the possible exception of me. But she knows the underground cities and I don't." Jack looked at Doug and shrugged. "Sorry Doug, but I don't think this works without her."

"But Cory's not here. He's used this portal to go to another city, and Christy hasn't seen it any more than any of us have," Doug countered, gesturing toward the portal setup that had taken Cory off.

"True, but just knowing what to expect in these cities, regardless of which particular one it is, may be the determining factor in finding him."

Doug opened his mouth to speak, but stopped himself. Crossing his arms defensively, he paused.

"No," he said finally, "it's too dangerous."

Jack squinted at him. "Let me guess. You were almost going to argue that Trevor has spent a lot of time in the city too, right?"

Doug smiled reluctantly. "I quickly realized saying that would not only be stupid but self-serving of me.

Trevor goes home too—no arguments." His smile was gone and he looked at Trevor and Christy defiantly.

Christy knew that he was digging in for a verbal fight and that he expected to take on all adversaries and come out on top. Before she could begin to argue, Trevor spoke up.

"I'm staying if Christy is. You're right that I know the city setup pretty well."

Christy's stomach tightened hearing Trevor talk. She knew what she had to say now, no matter what Trevor's reaction. But she realized once she spoke that he would think she was betraying him ... again. Empathy for him made her hesitate, but finally, even knowing what was coming, she said, "I'm staying. But you're right Dad, Trev has to go home."

"What! Come on, Christy! Again?" Shock and hurt showed plainly on his face.

Christy grabbed for his hand but he pulled it away.

"Trev, I couldn't have survived here without you, and you're the reason we have my dad back with us, but only one of us who knows anything about the cities needs to stay, and that's me. I almost got you killed or captured. Your mom must be going out of her mind not knowing what's happening." She paused, looking directly at him. "Even though I'm sure my mom has at least tried to calm your parents' fears, you need to go home. I don't want to be blamed for you as well as Cory."

When Trevor kept quiet, Christy turned to her dad. "I'm not leaving. You'd have to drag me into the portal and that's not going to happen. I'm needed here, Dad."

Doug didn't answer her. He turned away and wandered over to the impressive mural and stopped in front of it, staring. It was a map of the entire Empty World.

After a while, his head lowered. Without turning, he said softly, "Since when did my fourteen-year-old daughter start dictating terms to me? And since when did she start having such rational arguments that I had no choice but to agree with her?" He turned and faced the others. "But Trevor," he continued, "you are going back. End of discussion."

Trevor looked to Jack and the detective for support, but both of them nodded at Doug, agreeing with him.

"Not fair," Trevor mumbled.

Jack put his hand on Trevor's shoulder. "Son, there's nothing fair in this life at all. What you did to spring my son-in-law out of the Ancients' prison was nothing short of heroic, but your part in this is done. Has to be."

Trevor's shoulders slumped in resignation. "Then you need someone better than me, and even better than any of you. You can probably keep yourselves safe, but that doesn't mean you'll be able to meet the challenges you'll definitely find."

Christy stared at him, waiting for him to continue. Realizing he wasn't going to, she turned away and wandered off a few feet by herself. She needed to think.

Footsteps came up behind her. Her grandfather put his hand on her shoulder. "What's he talking about, Christy?"

"Brad. He means Brad."

Her grandfather frowned. "Why him?"

"Without Brad, none of us would have made it home. You saw him figure out the portal devices," she replied. "He also was the only one who was able to figure out how to get into the city through the hidden door mechanism. And he learned enough of Clacker's language to talk to him in a couple of hours or less. That's the most amazing thing I've ever seen. Brad might be the only one who would be able to see any challenges for what they really are and figure out how to overcome them."

Christy stepped back toward the group, realizing they were all listening in anyways, and continued explaining.

"There are a lot of tricks, like the walls and doors that don't appear to be walls or doors. The Ancients have set them up all over the place to protect themselves or to kill Cleaners. None of us see things the way Brad does. I will never ever call him strange again after what I saw him do. He may seem different to us because of his Asperger's, but if Brad was here, I'd feel a lot better. Even if it isn't fair to ask him to return any more than it's fair to make Trev leave."

She stopped, expecting someone to say something, but when nobody did, she added, "He was difficult and always seemed to be just about ready to cry or panic, but Danny mostly took the brunt of that and helped Brad through it when he could. And the more familiar Brad became with everything here, the better he was. Trev's the only one I told the whole story to. I didn't make Brad out to be a hero, but he was one."

Jack shook his head. "But he refused to come back this time, didn't he? What makes you think he'll change his mind? Even if his mom and dad would let him come back."

Christy thought for a moment. "He'll come if we make it clear that we'll never get Cory back without him. He worships Cory. Although I don't know why; Cory has teased, picked on and generally made his life more difficult nonstop. But I'm betting Mrs. Peters will let him. She's got to be dying worrying about Cory. I bet she'll be all for anything that will help bring Cory home. "

Jack nodded, accepting Christy's assessment, and immediately took charge.

"Then let's quickly decide who goes back for Brad with Trevor, because the longer we wait, the further away Cory could be getting."

"Wow. This looks just like the portal area I just left, but it's lit up more, not nearly as dark," Cory said. He'd gotten used to talking out loud when Murray was on his lap, and continued the habit even without the cat, whom he'd left behind for the others to take back to earth.

"Well, well, who do we have here? Someone in a mobile chair I see."

Cory spun his wheelchair around to face the voice addressing him.

"Sarynn?"

"No, my name is Tarynn. Who are you?"

"My name is Cory. I see you know English as well as Sarynn did."

The computer hologram seemed to smirk before she spoke. "You're not the first from your world to show up here. What happened to your legs?"

Cory wheeled a little closer and stopped. "For a computer you ask a lot of questions. You also look just like Sarynn in Vahuuldyn. But there's something different that I can't quite put my finger on."

"Ah, bright boy. I'm the newer version of Sarynn. When they decided to populate the cities with greeters in preparation for the return of our peoples, they started with Vahuuldyn and Sarynn. I'm of course here in Zaltruubanik and they upgraded my programming to evolve over time. I have a lot more personality than Sarynn. What do you think?" She spun around like she was showing off what she was wearing.

"I don't know. You do seem more animated … less computer-like, I guess. But Sarynn tried to make me laugh by playing a joke on me at one point, so you're not that different."

Tarynn frowned at Cory. "Not that different?" she asked, her voice cruel. "Oh, how wrong you are. But I'll give you the benefit of the doubt since you don't know me yet."

Cory instinctively wheeled back slightly at the tone in Tarynn's voice. *Not sure I want to know you better,* he thought. Tarynn seemed even angrier as Cory moved away from her.

"What? Did I scare you?" Tarynn's tone didn't soften in the least and Cory for the first time noticed her eyes. They were black and seemed to mirror the cruelty he heard in her voice.

Cory ignored her demeanor and instead got right down to what he'd come for.

"I'm looking for devices that make portals. I understand from Sarynn that they're manufactured here."

"Devices … portals … quaint terms, but I understand what you mean. Why do you need them?"

Despite Tarynns' attitude, Cory decided to be honest. "I want to try to find a world where they can heal my back so I can walk again."

"Seems a worthy reason to me." She smiled that cruel smile again. "But there is nothing here, I'm afraid, that can help you. Not because I wouldn't want to help, mind you," she continued, sounding delighted. "We ship all the components out to a small distribution center in a town called Boakly, so there hasn't been anything here for thousands of years."

"How do I get to the distribution center from here?"

She gestured at Cory in the wheelchair. "In that?" She pouted, tilting her head. "What a shame. I'm sure you can't traverse the terrain to get there."

Cory reacted to her condescending attitude. "What? You aren't advanced enough to send me there, wherever it is?"

"No, sorry," she said, not sounding the least bit sorry. "We don't have a portal to Boakly and the beltway there may not be functional. I don't have any knowledge of whether it is or not, but it's been a very long time. Just like I lost communication with Sarynn and Vahuuldyn, the link to Boakly and the distribution center has been down for ages."

Cory met those cruel eyes and Tarynn smiled again without any sympathy.

"Can I go take a look to see for myself?"

"Why certainly. Follow me." She gestured and started walking. "There's a functioning platform to the surface that brings you right out to the beltway area. But that platform won't come back down I'm afraid. Once it makes it to the surface, it is no longer under my control. Again, I warn you, I have no way of knowing if that beltway still functions. But the beltway's only destination is the distribution center, so if it is still working, you might get there. In any case, be warned that in that primitive contraption you use to get around with, I don't think you'll be able to get back here on your own once you're on the surface. But of course, it's up to you."

They entered a short alleyway and at the end of it was an open door. Tarynn pointed through it. "That is the platform. Enter that and I'll send you to the surface. The door won't close behind you. That got stuck a very long time ago, but it won't interfere with the function of the platform."

As Cory was wheeling around Tarynn to enter the platform, she spoke in a more monotone voice. "No, Darynn, I think not."

Cory stopped just short of entering the door. "What was that? Who is Darynn?"

Tarynn paused for a long few seconds, then said, "Darynn is my counterpart in Abuuenki. The link there has never been lost. She was just asking me a question, that's all. She's very pushy, bordering on nosy, and listens in on me all the time." She trained that cruel smile on Cory again. "Get in."

Cory wheeled in and turned to watch Tarynn. "You sure this takes me to the surface?"

"Of course. I wouldn't lie to you."

I wouldn't put it past you, Cory thought.

"I'll start it up now." Tarynn frowned, this time a legitimate one. "It's taking a bit longer than I thought. It has sat for centuries. Give it a second and it may ascend slowly."

Finally the platform began slowly to rise up. Cory thought of something. "There may be some others who come looking for me."

The platform stopped. "What do you mean? What others?"

"I have some friends who may come looking for me. You can tell them I'm okay and it probably would be alright to let them follow me. At this point, they can't stop me."

"Are they in wheelchairs like you?"

"No, of course not."

Tarynn smiled that icy smile and started the platform.

As Cory rose up, almost out of sight, he heard Tarynn say in that monotone voice, "No, Darynn, he'd be useless to you, but I may have other options soon."

CHAPTER 2

"Just because I said I'd feel a whole lot better if Brad were here, doesn't mean I want him to come back, even if he would want to," Christy explained. "Without Danny to help him, Brad would be a lot to deal with and I'd have to worry about him again." She paced the room, and Trevor stepped in front of her to cut her off, holding up his hands.

"Christy, you aren't responsible for him or any of us. Just because, years ago, you were the first to know that your grandfather was stranded here, doesn't mean the rest of what's happened since is your fault. Stop blaming yourself."

Jack nodded agreement. "Your grandmother should never have told you about this place. Me being selfish and continuing to return here until the portal eventually stopped working and stranded me ... that's the real start of this. And that's on me."

"No, Grandpa, you and Trev are both wrong. I caused Rob to come here and lose his hearing, and then Cory broke his back, and both of you," she said, looking at her dad and then the detective, "got lost here coming after me, and then you, Dad, were captured for months. If I hadn't been standing on the dock waiting for the lightning that night, none of this would have happened. None of it."

"Assigning blame can stop right now," Detective Lockhart said. "We have to get moving and decide what we're going to do. And to that end, I'll go back with Trevor to talk to the Peters, since I was Wendel's boss years ago. That makes the most sense."

Everyone nodded. "Good," Jack said, "I think one of us should stay back here and wait for Mike to return, hopefully with Brad. The other two should go after Cory as quickly as possible."

"I should go with grandpa while you stay and wait, Dad," Christy said. "We have the best chance together."

Jack shook his head. "No, Christy. Even though that makes a lot of sense, you and your dad should hurry up and go after Cory. It makes more sense for me to stay back and wait so that, when Mike returns with or without Brad, there'll be one of us in each group who's most familiar with this world."

Trevor looked uncomfortable and was shifting his weight from one foot to the other.

"There you go again, Trev. What is it?" Christy asked.

"I don't think you guys should separate. You should wait for Detective Lockhart to return, with or without Brad. Splitting up is a bad idea. We don't know how long ago Cory went through this portal here, so speed may be less important than all of you being together."

Jack paced. "Trevor makes a very good point," he said finally. "As much as I hate waiting, it does make more sense. We have strength in numbers"

After many nods of agreement, it was settled.

"What about Murray?" Trevor asked, picking up the cat that'd been slinking around his feet.

"Take him back to earth with you," Jack said.

Just then, as if on cue, Murray hissed and scratched Trevor. Trevor dropped him, and Murray scurried off and disappeared around a corner.

"Never mind him then if he's going to be temperamental," Jack said.

"Wait two seconds," Christy said, removing a small digital camera from her pack. She started on one wall and took two quick pictures of the murals that decorated the massive room they were in. The murals depicted stunning scenes of life from the city's past.

A major portion of one of the murals was a map depicting the whole planet.

It showed crisscrossing lines for transportation routes, squares that represented cities, and various strange symbols and graphs. Clearly the structures on the map were now long gone or in ruins; they hadn't seen anything on the surface of the planet except for an endless expanse of tan moss, the occasional hill, and primitive structures. Most of what was remaining now had probably been built long after the civilization had crumbled.

Christy checked that her pictures were clear and put the camera away again. She shrugged at the stares. "You never know when that map might come in handy. It looks like it's the whole world here."

Trevor laughed. "How come I didn't know you had that camera with you?"

Christy grinned. "I was so mean to Cory when he brought out his camera when we were traveling together that I felt awkward letting anyone know I had one with me. Especially when Cory was with us."

Christy set down her pack and got busy connecting the four devices to build the portal and inserting three of the crystals, keeping the fourth one out. She set the four ceramic cups down in a square.

"Detective Lockhart, you and Trev need to get into the square," Christy directed. "Wait a minute," she said, suddenly stopping short. Everyone looked at her in confusion.

"What's the matter, Christy?" Jack asked.

Christy held up one finger, gesturing for them to continue to wait. "Sarynn? Are you listening?"

The computer projection of an Ancient girl appeared. "What do you want? You've been rude to me, you know."

Christy waved off the comment. "Can you tell us how to set these devices to return right to this spot? There must be a setting in here to do that. Brad came close, setting it to come back to the city, but not close enough. We need it to come right back here."

"You're pushing your luck, young lady. But since you did save my world and everything in it from a swift and almost certain death, I'll help you."

Christy turned to Trevor. He was shaking his head at the computer's attitude. "Zip it, Trev," Christy whispered.

Sarynn bent down next to the four connected devices, motioning for Christy to join her, and pointed to a small sliding mechanism in one of them.

"Move that three notches over." She waited as Christy complied. "Good. Now press down on that switch." She pointed again and Christy did as she was instructed.

"Good. Now turn that dial— right there, next to that switch you just pressed— three and a half turns."

Christy did it and Sarynn nodded. "Ok, you're good to go."

"Thank you, Sarynn."

"We're even now, don't you think?" Sarynn said smugly.

Trevor guffawed. "*Even?* Not even close, Pixel Lady," Trevor said. It was a name he'd picked up from Cory.

"Nobody asked you, did they?" Sarynn challenged, staring coldly at Trevor.

Christy stepped between them, staring Trevor down for a second before turning to the computer projection. "We really do appreciate the help. If you want to call us 'even,' I'm ok with that."

"Fine, I'm outta here." Sarynn blinked-out immediately, without another word.

"That computer could use an attitude upgrade," Doug offered.

"Let's hurry," Jack prompted them.

Trevor jumped out of the square and over to Christy. She grabbed him and held on. "Thank you, you're the best," she whispered in his ear.

Trevor stepped back, wiping his eyes. He reached in his pocket and took out a small plastic bottle, handing it to Christy.

"It's the rest of the Ibuprofen. Your ankle may need it still," he said.

Christy inserted the final crystal and the connected devices began to hum. As the wall of light built up along the outer rim of the square of cups and then shifted just inside of them as it built height, Christy separated the devices, collapsing them and storing them in an empty backpack. Then she handed the pack to Trevor and stepped back, blowing a kiss toward him and the detective. Seconds later, the two were gone and the portal had dissipated.

The platform was like an elevator without walls or a ceiling, which was a little scary as it ascended. It rose through a shaft with only faint, occasional points of light. Cory tried counting the levels to take his mind off his nervousness, but he couldn't find any reference points. Finally the platform slowed as it neared what he hoped was the surface. He watched as the ceiling came slowly closer and hoped the platform would stop before it crushed him against the ceiling. The platform did stop finally and bright light shone through the bottom edge of what looked like a door. *That better be daylight, otherwise I'm not all the way up to the surface*, he thought. *Wherever I am, this doesn't go any higher, so I need to get out.*

Cory wheeled forward a few steps and the door began making horrible grinding sounds. It startled him so much that he put his hands over his ears until the noises lessened, and the door, with one final tearing sound, opened three quarters of the way and stopped. Cory slowly removed his hands from his ears and wheeled tentatively towards the opening. There was just enough room for him to squeeze his wheelchair out. Squinting in the bright light of the surface, he came out to a ruined, unfamiliar world.

There was none of the tan moss that had dominated the landscape Cory was so used to seeing. This part of the Empty World hadn't been reclaimed by that yet. Here, the earth was bare, with intermittent tufts of a thick, vomit-yellow grass poking up from it. All around him was crumbling concrete, or at least that's what it resembled. This was still the nearly dead and decaying remains of the past civilization of the Ancients. Partial rails and wall-structures were everywhere and stretched off into the distance; some sections were missing, and some were just gleaming rods of metal without their coating of that crumbling concrete-like material. The remains of foundations were close by. They'd crumbled to the point where only the faintest hint was still above ground. Adding to the barren impression, no debilitating sound or hurricane-force wind disturbed the ruins. Cory had never seen the surface without that wind before. He wondered if it was because of what he and Trevor had done, or if perhaps it just wasn't part of the weather where he now found himself.

Tarynn said there should be a working beltway around here somewhere. Cory looked down and was relieved to see that the remains of some pavement led away from the platform. Large cracks and loose debris were scattered over the surface, but it looked as if, for the most part, he'd be able to maneuver over it if he was careful in choosing his path.

Wheeling out onto the road, he started his search. Without the wind and noise, it quickly became clear that there was something causing a hum in the air.

Could be the beltway. Cory slowly picked his way toward where the hum seemed to originate. It was tough going, always having to zig and zag around breaks in the concrete. Cory stopped and peered down into a wide, dark crack in the ground. Not seeing the bottom, he reached down and picked up a fist-sized rock and dropped it into the gap. He waited to hear it hit but detected no sound. *Maybe there's soft sand at the bottom,* Cory thought. He was still frowning at the puzzle when he heard a rustling coming from the crack and instinctively backed up just in time. Spider-like critters the size of golf balls poured out of the opening in a stream. Dozens scattered across the pavement, spreading out and enveloping anything in their path.

"Whoa. Creepy." Cory backed up further and still had to swivel his chair to keep some of them from crawling up his legs.

He watched as the mass of critters reformed a few yards away. Suddenly, as if they were one entity, they surged and flowed over the ground, avoiding the obstacles and showing Cory a safe path he could take.

When the creatures were no longer in sight, he wheeled off along the path they'd taken. A parting gift was the ugly, dark stain they'd left in their path as they scurried away. It was almost like having the lighted path from Sarynn. *Only more organic.* Cory smiled at the thought. He followed the creatures and when he too wheeled over the small rise, he saw a moving beltway, glistening ribbon-like in the sunshine and winding off into the distance

The belt was twenty yards wide and appeared to be made of crystallized rubber. It was amazing to him that it had continued to function after the rest of the civilization had crumbled. *But why does it only go in one direction?* he wondered. It didn't make sense to him.

There should be another beltway running parallel to this but heading in the other direction, he thought.

Well, Tarynn did say it only goes to Boakly, so if I get on it, I can't get lost. Cory shrugged, and taking a deep breath, slid from the platform onto the beltway. It took a few seconds to steady himself, but then he turned to face forward and let the road take him.

Pretty soon he'd figured out how the beltway was constructed, how it managed to turn corners or slowly drift in one direction or the other when it seemed to be one long, continuous beltway. It wasn't continuous at all; it was a series of sections. Only a very tiny bump was felt each time he went on to the next section. Despite the strangeness of the road itself, and the unfamiliar landscape that looked more like a warzone than the monotonous tan moss and clumped vegetation he'd spent days trudging through months before, the anticipation of what he hoped to find up ahead excited him.

CHAPTER 3

Detective Lockhart and Trevor had both changed into dry clothes after their emergence into Christy's pond where the portal had dumped them. They had gone first to see Christy's mom, and then to see Trevor's to explain their mission. Now, talking to the Peters was all that was left to do.

Trevor was very quiet in the passenger seat. The reunion with his mom had been emotional.

Detective Lockhart looked over at him. "I know this is hard for you. I suspect that even though you're back home now, somehow, your part in all this isn't over, even though Jack said that it was. I think it was said just to emphasize you needed to come home."

"Feels over to me."

Lockhart smiled at the grumpy response. He understood Trevor's bitterness and let him sit silently for the few minutes it took to get to the Peters' house.

"I'd appreciate you coming in with me to talk to Mrs. Peters. It may make a big difference," Lockhart said as he shut off the car and opened his door.

Trevor nodded without any enthusiasm, but he got out of the passenger's side and walked silently up to the front door with the detective.

Before they could even knock, Mrs. Peters had flung the door wide open and exclaimed, "Trevor! You're back! Where's Cory? Is he ok?" She was almost screaming as she looked from Trevor to the detective, waiting for answers.

"As far as we know, he's fine," Lockhart replied, gesturing with his hands up for her to settle down. "Let's go inside and we'll explain," he added.

Mrs. Peters looked confused and scared. Before letting them come in, she said, "What do you mean, 'as far as you know'?"

"Please, let's go in and sit. We'll tell you everything." Lockhart motioned toward the living room.

"Quickly then, come in and sit down." She didn't wait for any response, just turned and headed for her living room, assuming they'd follow, which they did.

As Cory got closer to Boakly, he began to see signs that the town was still there. After traveling through nothing but ruins since reaching the surface of Zyltruubanik, he'd been worried that the town would be a ruin too.

Buildings came into view as he slowly let the beltway carry him forward. His excitement was growing. But something looked funny up ahead. About a hundred yards ahead, the beltway wasn't moving. He had no choice but to let himself be carried to that section, and despite it not moving, he was propelled onto it by the preceding one. He manually wheeled himself forward. There was quite a bit of debris on this non-moving section, but the next section, only a hundred yards or so ahead, was working fine, so he maneuvered around them.

He made it back onto the functioning beltway and let it pull him, hoping that there wouldn't be any more broken sections ahead.

As he approached the town, Cory noticed it didn't look quite as appealing as it had from a distance. First, he couldn't see any signs of activity even though lights gleamed to illuminate the streets. That seemed odd to him, given that it was daytime. Secondly, the town, although not exactly a ruin, was most certainly not in its heyday.

The structures he could make out seemed to have superfluous construction on top of the roofs and jutting out from the sides of them. And the extra construction didn't look anything like the sophisticated buildings and rooms he'd seen in the cities. These add-ons were seemingly made of wood, perhaps something even less permanent, and followed no obvious pattern. It looked like the town had been rebuilt right on top of the original one, but the work was shoddy at best.

Cory let himself be carried to it despite his misgivings. Here the moss began to creep over much of the ruins as if trying to reclaim the land, which was terrain that Cory was familiar with. When he was just about to be carried onto what looked like the last quarter mile of beltway, he encountered another stretch that wasn't working.

Wheeling onto it, he looked for any signs of life ahead or anything else he could identify as either helpful or a possible threat. Not seeing either, he was just about to proceed when a noise to the right of the beltway startled him.

He quickly spun his chair to face the sound. Among the moss and the rubble of ruined pavement, an eight-foot square section of the ruins was lifting up out of the ground like a lid being opened. A squeaking noise announced that the hinges were not often utilized or lubricated.

Cory watched as first a head, then a body rose up out of the hole.

When the top half of the figure was fully visible, Cory was surprised to see it was a Garlian and definitely a girl. She motioned for Cory to come toward her. It was the same gesture that the Garlians in Vahuuldyn had used to get him to follow them. This time there was the problem of how? The ruined pavement between him and the opening was littered with debris, and moss had reclaimed some of it.

Cory hoped that since she was using gestures, she'd understand him as he threw up his hands in helplessness and pointed first to the obstacle-strewn path between them and then to his wheelchair.

The girl rose further out of the opening and nodded.

"I'll come for you and help," she said in perfect English.

"Brad, can you come down here?" Mrs. Peters yelled up to her son. Detective Lockhart had explained everything to the nervous and crying woman with an occasional comment from Trevor.

"Are you certain we shouldn't wait for Wendel to come home?" Lockhart asked.

Mrs. Peters snorted her distain as she shook her head. "He'll only try to turn this to his advantage somehow. I don't see how, but he'd try."

Lockhart nodded as they heard Brad come down the stairs and walk into the room.

"Brad, you know Trevor and should remember Detective Lockhart."

Brad listened to his mom and quickly glanced at the visitors before setting his eyes firmly on the floor at his feet.

Mrs. Peters' tone softened as she started to explain. "Cory's still missing, Brad, and we think you can help us find him."

"No, no, no." Brad spun around and started to bolt for the door.

"Don't you dare do that, Brad." Mrs. Peters had changed her tone dramatically and it stopped Brad in his tracks.

"Turn around so we can see your face please, Brad." Mrs. Peters had said please but it was clearly a command.

Brad turned and again focused on his feet. Mrs. Peters nodded at the detective and Trevor before she addressed her son again in her quiet voice. "Without your help, we may never see Cory again. You don't want that, do you, Brad?"

Brad shook his head and pouted but kept silent. He was fidgety and started wringing his hands together, obviously wishing he could leave the room. "I don't like that place," he finally began. "Bad people wanted to hurt me and Danny. I'm not going back." Brad never took his eyes off the floor as he spoke.

Mrs. Peters started to cry.

"Brad, look at me, please." He looked up and she continued. "You're the only hope. You have to do this for Cory."

Brad shook his head and squatted down, resting his elbows on his knees. He covered his face with his hands and began rocking gently.

"No, no, no, no, no," he said. "Never again, never again."

Mrs. Peters looked at the detective with a resigned and hopeless expression.

Lockhart shook his head. "I guess that's it then." He stood up, but Trevor motioned for him to come close and whispered in his ear. The detective nodded.

"Brad," Lockhart began. "What if we could get Danny to go with you? Would you consider it then?"

Brad continued to rock with his face hidden in his hands but said, "I'll go with Danny. But Danny won't go. He never wants to see that place again. That's what he said."

Detective Lockhart nodded and turned to Trevor. "I'll drop you back at home then head to Danny's house and see if I can convince him and his mom to let him go back."

Brad stopped rocking. "He never wants to go to that place again," he repeated. "That's what he said."

The girl came toward the beltway and stopped right at its edge. "Come here. Quickly now!"

Cory wheeled forward and stopped with the Garlian right in front of him. She took hold of the wheels and slowly moved them so that the chair slipped down off of the beltway. It plopped down onto the ruined pavement with just a small jolt as she took as much of the weight as she could.

When Cory was completely off the beltway, the girl pulled his chair forward a couple of feet and stepped behind it. She began pushing him towards the opening she'd come out of. As they got closer to it, Cory saw it wasn't just a hole. It was a ramp that led underground.

As he was pushed through the opening, he descended quickly into the ground and the surface landscape disappeared from view. Within a few seconds, they came to a level section and the girl closed the lid behind them, leaving them in the dark.

Cory heard her footsteps as she returned and started pushing again. "Light is just up ahead. Be patient. And stay silent." It was an order.

'Just up ahead' was a relative term, apparently. Cory had to exercise that patience the girl spoke of as he was pushed through complete darkness for several long minutes.

During that time, Cory berated himself for trusting this unknown Garlian and letting her take charge.

After too long a time in silence, Cory was about to disobey the Garlian and speak, when light came into view up ahead.

Instead of heading toward it, the girl grunted something under her breath as the sound of footsteps echoed toward them. Quickly spinning Cory's chair around, the girl retreated into the darkness, and then, even though he couldn't see it, she pushed the two of them into a side passage and stopped.

Cory felt her breath on his cheek as she leaned over and whispered in his ear, "If you value your life, silence."

"This isn't fair. I don't care if Cory ever comes back. He deserves whatever happens to him." Danny stomped his feet as he signed and spoke to his mom and the detective.

"Danny, honey, you don't mean that." Katie Lake spoke for Detective Lockhart's benefit as she signed to her son.

Danny stared defiantly at his mom without responding.

Finally, the detective broke the awkward standoff. Staring right at Danny so the boy could read his lips, he said, "Brad feels so comfortable with you. You have become an amazing friend to him. I wish I could say that Brad will go without you, but he won't. Knowing him as you now do, you know when he says he won't go if you don't go with him, he means it."

Katie signed the detective's comments just to make sure that Danny had understood, but he turned away from both of them. His shoulders began to shake up and down as he sobbed.

"For anyone but Cory, I'd think about it, but he doesn't deserve any help," Danny said aloud through his tears. He turned to talk directly to the detective. "You know he started this whole mess by pushing Rob into the pond and laughing about it? He's selfish and cares about only himself."

Seeing the detective was at a loss for what to say, Katie stepped into her son's view and signed as she spoke.

"Yes, he's not been the best friend to anyone so far, but that doesn't mean we shouldn't help as much as we can. I don't want you to go at all, honey, but I see that

Brad may be critical to Cory's rescue and that means you are needed too." Katie too began to cry as she finished speaking and turned to the detective standing next to her, and buried her head on his shoulder.

Lockhart seemed startled, but instinctively wrapped an arm around her. "Danny's right, though," she said. "This isn't fair at all. He can't see my lips, so he doesn't know that I agree with him in principle. It's terrible that he's been put into this predicament. I'll try to keep convincing him to go, but only if you, Detective, promise me you'll do everything you can to protect him."

She stepped back out of the detective's comforting embrace and stared at him.

"Of course I will, as will Doug Walker and Jack Renfrew. You have my word."

Katie nodded at the detective's words and smiled sadly.

"What was that about?" Danny asked aloud.

Katie turned and knelt down in front of him. "Nobody wants to go back to the Empty World. I'm sure Brad is terribly afraid of going back, but he's willing to as long as you go with him. Imagine me, honey. How do you think I feel standing here giving you permission to go back? That is the last thing I want to do. But Cory needs you and Brad. And remember, the detective, Christy's dad, and her grandfather are all going to be there with you."

Danny turned away again from his mom.

"I have no choice, do I?" he asked angrily. Facing the two adults, he said again, "This isn't fair."

Danny was silent all the way over to the Peters' house. When they walked in, Mrs. Peters hugged him, crying with relief that he'd agreed to go with Brad to rescue Cory. Seeing Brad again and the grateful reaction of Mrs. Peters helped him feel a bit better as they enabled the devices. Mrs. Peters was wide eyed with wonder and fear as they stepped into the portal in front of her and dissolved back to the Empty World.

CHAPTER 4

"Ok, listen up!" Jack yelled above the confusion and excitement as everyone greeted each other. The noise gradually stopped and everyone looked to him.

"Now that Danny and Brad are here with us, let's get going."

Christy nodded and slipped the crystals into the portal devices that were set up at the sides of the room that Sarynn had told them was a portal to the city of Zyltruubanik. Then she joined everyone, hugging Danny as she crowded in with the rest of them. Suddenly, just before the portal fully activated, Murray the cat lunged into the square with them, as if from out of thin air.

Tarynn flashed into view as the group materialized in Zyltruubanik.

"Well, what have we here? Apparently Cory was correct."

Jack spoke first. "So you've seen Cory?"

"Not so fast. We haven't had formal introductions yet. I'm Tarynn."

Jack was about to respond when Tarynn stopped him. "You'll go last for speaking before I even told you my name."

Detective Lockhart held up his hand to stop Jack from reacting angrily. Then he bowed and said, "Hello, Tarynn, I'm Mike Lockhart, and this is—"

"Uh uh, each must speak for themselves," Tarynn commanded.

"Hello, I'm Christy Walker," Christy announced. She signed as well, so that Danny would understand introductions were taking place. He struggled to read Ancients' lips.

"What was that all about? Keep your hands by your side." Tarynn's voice took on a hard edge, ripe with annoyance.

Taking a cue from Mike Lockhart, Doug bowed slightly. "I'm Doug Walker."

Danny nodded, smiling at Christy, and said, "Hello, I'm Danny Lake."

"What's with the funny speech, kid?" Tarynn asked, expertly mocking the sound of Danny's voice.

Christy took a step forward, wanting to say something, but her dad stopped her with a look. She grunted, frustrated, but kept quiet, opting to just watch Tarynn who was smiling without any warmth to her eyes. She was very different than Sarynn. Christy felt uncomfortable with the whole exchange, surprised at how demanding the holographic girl was. Just then, out of the corner of her eye, Christy saw Murray bolt away from the group and disappear around a corner.

"I've seen those creatures before. Useless bunches of fur," Tarynn said, her eyes following the cat until it was gone. She then began walking slowly around the group and stopped in front of Brad, marveling at how he was staring at his own feet, as usual.

"Who are you?" Tarynn asked coldly.

Christy began to answer. "That's Bra—"

"I asked him, not you," Tarynn snapped.

"He may not respond," Jack interrupted. "His name is Brad."

Tarynn's eyes widened as she turned to Jack. But he was staring back defiantly, his arms crossed over his chest.

Tarynn met Jack's eyes momentarily before turning again to stare at Brad.

"No matter." She dismissed the confrontation with a wave.

"I'm Jack. What was it you said about Cory?"

"He said he might be followed."

"So he's here," Christy said.

"Was here." Tarynn grinned coldly. "He's in Abuuenki looking for what you call portal devices. I sent him there."

Christy was about to say something when Jack held up his hand, halting her.

"Ok, Tarynn," he began. "Can we get to Abuuenki too? Is that another city?" He folded his arms and held Tarynn's glare.

Christy was momentarily annoyed with her grandfather for cutting her off, but she realized that he had potentially figured out how to deal with the holograph to get the best responses.

"I can send you there to find Cory. Yes, it is a city." Tarynn's voice became less hard, more conciliatory.

"How do we get there?" Jack asked.

Christy watched the back and forth and suddenly felt a tug on her sleeve. She turned and it was Brad. When she looked at him, he dropped his eye contact. But contrary to his aversion to physical contact, he kept tugging on her sleeve.

She frowned, wondering at the unusual behavior and whispered to him.

"What is it, Brad?"

Brad kept his contact, pulling gently on her sleeve as he stepped back. After glancing quickly at Tarynn, he dropped his eyes again.

Christy moved with him a step and he responded by stepping back two more paces, pulling Christy with him.

Glancing quickly at Tarynn again, Brad mumbled something.

Christy leaned in, not sure what he'd said. "What was that, Brad?" she whispered.

He shifted his eyes to Tarynn repeatedly then met Christy's eyes and said, barely above a whisper, "Cory's not there. Tarynn is lying."

Footsteps and wavering light approached them as Cory and the mysterious Garlian girl hid in the side passage. Cory felt himself pushed farther in until they turned around a bend and stopped once more. The girl spun him around. Footsteps echoed back in the main tunnel, but any light was swallowed up by the darkness and distance.

Suddenly, light flicked off the walls and the girl mumbled something under her breath in a language Cory couldn't understand. Faint voices mingled with the sound of footsteps, but the light disappeared. They remained there in complete darkness for what seemed a very long time until the footsteps and voices could no longer be heard.

"I think they've gone," the girl stated.

Cory was getting a little annoyed with the way things were going. "Who are they?" he asked.

"They run Boakly."

"So? Why are we hiding? What did you mean, 'value my life'?"

"You would be useless to them and would be killed. I, on the other hand, would be taken as a slave. But in the end, my fate would be the same as yours, just delayed for as long as I proved useful."

"Boy, the more I get around! This world is anything but empty."

"Huh?"

Cory smiled in the dark. "Never mind. Why are you worried about being captured and made a slave?"

"Those who inhabit Boakly have set up a caste system. Many of us were slaves there. We who object have escaped to the tunnels and the hidden arenas that our ancestors dug thousands of years ago. We have made our own life here below the city, but some of those above know some of these tunnels and they come down in raiding parties to find more slaves. Each passing year they find more of our tunnels."

Cory could hear the anger in her voice. "Why don't you just leave?"

"Some of us have, but the rest of us stay to try and free those of us who have been enslaved. We have our own raiding parties and it is our mission to free as many of our kind as we can. It's a losing battle but we keep on."

"Great. So you don't even live in the city above?"

"No, only those of us who are slaves."

Cory slapped his thighs in frustration. "So much for me finding devices then."

"What do you mean?"

He took a deep breath, realizing that he didn't even know who he was talking to. "My name is Cory. What's yours?"

"I'm Ufei."

"You speak English very well."

Ufei sighed. "During my father's time, he freed a human who remained with us for the rest of his life. He taught all of us his language. It comes in handy when we raid. Those in Boakly don't know your language so we can communicate with many of the slaves of our kind without them knowing what we're saying."

Cory was only partly listening to the girl. His mind was racing. What was he going to do now? How was he going to get back with the beltway running in only one direction? He needed to get back to the portal in Zyltruubanik. There was nothing he could do here now to find more devices. Even if he could get back to the platform that had taken him up to the surface, Tarynn had said that he'd never be able to get back down into the city.

"Ufei? How do I get back to where I came from?"

Ufei didn't answer right away. Finally she said, "Wait a minute. I'll be right back."

Before Cory could object, she was gone, her footsteps receding. He heard her slap the wall and chant something rhythmic. Her footsteps came forward again and she repeated the exercise a second time. Suddenly the tunnel was filled with light. Ufei was standing a few feet away and smiled with her pencil thin mouth.

"What did you do?"

Ufei reached into a pocket in her flowing coat and removed a crystal, holding it up for Cory to see. "We light these tunnels with them. I needed to find the receptacle by counting a certain number of steps in the dark. Then I inserted a crystal."

"So that's how the tunnels are lighted. I've never seen the source before in any of the tunnels I've been in, must have missed the receptacles with the crystals."

Ufei opened her mouth to speak, but just at that moment an echoing tap came down the tunnel. The girl listened for a second, then stepped toward Cory and began pushing quickly.

"What's going on?"

"We need to go. I've been summoned."

"Summoned? By who?" Cory craned his neck to look at Ufei as she pushed him through the now lighted tunnel, but she ignored his question, so they moved in silence until finally emerging into the main tunnel again, which was also newly illuminated. Another Garlian was standing there, young like Ufei, but a male.

"Cory, this is my friend Tyncil."

The boy nodded to Cory and raised an eyebrow above one of his small black eyes to Ufei.

The girl dismissed it with a wave. "Long story, not now. What's up?"

"They've got Abei."

Ufei gasped. "No! How?"

"He was part of a raid that went bad. They freed nobody and Abei was captured." Tyncil reached a hand and placed it on Ufei's shoulder. "We'll get him back."

"Not if they find out who he is," Ufei said bitterly, beginning to cry.

Cory couldn't stand it anymore. "Who's Abei?"

Tyncil kept quiet so Ufei sobbed an answer. "Our leader's son, and my brother."

"You know Abei almost as well as I do, Tyncil," Ufei said through her sobs. "He has always taken advantage of our status as the Leader's children. Do you not think he'll let those above know who he is?"

"You are probably correct, Ufei. We must go back to the group and discuss what's to be done. We have to act before Abei gives away his status if we have any chance of success." Tyncil pointed to Cory and then raised an eyebrow again.

Ufei smiled grimly. "He must come with us."

Tyncil shook his head.

"We can't leave him to die," Ufei protested.

Tyncil stared at her for a moment then shrugged.

"I will push the human, Tyncil. You remove the crystals and catch up."

Even before Cory could see if Tyncil had agreed, Ufei was pushing him rapidly through the tunnels. Within a few seconds, all went dark again, but Cory never felt his progress slow.

Rushing silently along the pitch black tunnels, the only sound that of Ufei's labored breathing, Cory was truly afraid for what was in store for him.

Minutes after their flight had begun, Cory sensed that Tyncil had silently caught up. Maybe it was the faint sound of the Garlian's breathing or maybe it was just that innate sense that people have where they can feel the presence of another person, even in the dark. His fear gradually lessened and was replaced by respect and amazement at the Garlians' ability to maneuver through complete darkness.

After what seemed like an hour (but was probably less than a third of that), the tunnel began to lighten.

Ufei finally slowed down and stopped. Both Garlians leaned against the tunnel walls, their chests heaving as they gulped air.

"We are relatively safe from here on out, so we can walk the rest of the way," Ufei explained as she resumed pushing. Her sobbing had stopped and had been replaced by anger, which revealed her concern over her brother's capture.

After being pushed in silence for a few minutes more, Cory was wheeled through an open doorway and into a large room, which was much more brightly lit and filled with a dozen Garlians.

Ufei pushed Cory to the center of the room and stopped. Garlians surrounded him immediately. They were wearing the exact same blue flowing coats that Cory was familiar with. Some of them were male, some were female, but all of them were young. There didn't seem to be an adult in the lot of them.

Ufei stepped from behind Cory's chair and put a hand on his shoulder. "This is Cory," she said. "I had to take him into the tunnels before he reached Boakly."

Nods from all the Garlians told Cory that each of them knew the danger.

Tyncil pointed at four of the Garlians. "You will be the rescue team."

Three males and one female nodded and separated themselves from the others.

Cory watched for what would happen next, expecting someone to say something, but all were silent. Finally, one of the members of the rescue team spoke up. "I will do it."

Tyncil placed his hand on the Garlian's shoulder. "Thank you, Panfei. May your courage and your feet not fail you."

Ufei went to the Garlian and hugged him quickly, and the other three Garlians who'd been chosen clasped Panfei on the shoulder.

"Go quickly, now. You know where Abei has been taken," Tyncil said.

The four left without another word or glance

After a moment, Ufei resumed introductions, but Cory interrupted her.

"What did Panfei mean when he said 'I will do it'?" he asked.

Ufei answered slowly. "When we go on a rescue mission, if we free some of our enslaved friends, we will be pursued. We can't allow any from above to follow us to our living quarters here in the tunnels. To keep our locations secret, one of the rescue team must create a diversion as best they can so the rest can get back to us without giving away where we are."

Cory wondered why Ufei seemed so reluctant to answer. "What do you mean 'create a diversion'?"

Ufei cleared her throat, hesitating before she continued. "It usually means allowing oneself to be captured."

Cory put his hands up to his head and moaned. "So to rescue someone, someone else has to be sacrificed?"

CHAPTER 5

"**W**hy would she lie?" Christy asked loud enough for only Brad to hear. She didn't really expect an answer, and when Brad dropped eye contact, she knew for sure one wasn't coming.

"How do you know she's lying?" Christy asked, trying again.

Silence.

Brad looked at Tarynn, who was still talking with Jack, then dropped his eyes once more.

"Please, Brad, answer me," Christy whispered, tugging on his sleeve.

"The colors around her."

Christy frowned. She knew Brad had answered her but if she was going to get anything useful out of that answer, she'd have to keep asking questions.

"Colors?" she said aloud, searching for anything she could try to trigger more of a response from Brad. "What about the colors? I don't see any colors around her, but you do, I guess." She tugged on his sleeve again. "Something is different about the colors around her when she lies? Is that it?"

Brad smiled one of the few smiles she'd ever seen from him and he nodded. "The colors change."

Just then, her dad came over to them. "Christy, Brad, come on. Tarynn is going to activate the portal to the city Cory went to."

Brad started to shake his head. "No, no, no."

"What's his problem?" Tarynn snapped.

Christy faced Brad and leaned in, forehead to forehead. "Brad, let's go. Tell me more when we've gotten to the city, ok?"

Brad shook his head again but Christy insisted. "Let's go, Brad. I promise we'll stop and listen as soon as we get there."

Jack waved everyone over and Brad followed Christy. Suddenly an idea struck her. "I'm going to ask Tarynn something," she whispered to Brad. "Watch to see if it's the truth, ok?"

Brad made eye contact for a split second.

"Tarynn?" Christy looked at the girl.

"What?" She sounded really annoyed.

"Can you show me where this city is that we're in and also where Abuuenki is? I have a picture of the mural in Vahuuldyn."

Tarynn hesitated then said, "I suppose so."

Christy took out her camera for Tarynn to see.

"How is the information stored?"

Christy fumbled momentarily and removed the sim card, holding that up.

"I see that there are contact points, very primitive, but I'll interface with them."

Immediately a two dimensional screen appeared with all the pictures on the sim card set in holographic rows.

"Which picture are you referring to?"

Christy pointed and the screen changed to the mural picture, expanding to twice the size of the original projection.

Tarynn then showed them by lighting up on the mural screen where first Vahuuldyn was, then where Abuuenki was and finally where they were now, in Zyltruubanik.

"Thank you, Tarynn." Christy was about to say something more but Tarynn waved her to silence.

"I haven't got all day. Let's go!"

As they prepared themselves for the portal journey, Detective Lockhart spoke up. "You can set this to get us to Abuuenki, not back to Vahuuldyn?"

"Already done. One of you just has to put the crystals in place," Tarynn said.

Jack quickly did it and the portal began generating.

Tarynn stood outside the square, her lips set into that cold grin. As the wall of light grew, a chill ran through Christy as she noticed Tarynn's face take on a blank stare. Then Tarynn laughed and said, "Of course, Darynn, don't be so impatient. They're all yours. You're welcome. Just remember, you owe me."

"It's how we've always done things. Usually we come out ahead if we rescue more than one Garlian," Ufei said, defending their strategy for how they freed their fellow Garlians.

The other Garlians in the room were nodding their agreement.

"There's got to be a better way," Cory argued. "You just sent four people to rescue one person and fully expect one of those four to be captured after you free Abei. That's one for one, makes no sense at all."

"There is hope that Panfei can escape too, but he knows his first priority is to make sure no one from above can follow the rest of the rescue party," Tyncil said, supporting Ufei.

"Does that ever happen? Does anyone ever get away after making sure that those from the city can't follow your rescue party back to here?" Cory challenged.

Ufei dropped her eyes. "No, not ever."

"So you just traded Panfei for Abei. And that's assuming your raid is successful. How often do you lose some or all of a rescue party without freeing anyone?"

Nobody answered right away, so Cory wheeled his chair right up to Ufei, who backed off a step.

"Since nobody is volunteering an answer, my guess is that it happens a lot."

Cory stared at each of the Garlians in turn, waiting for one of them to protest or correct him.

Tyncil nodded, looking uncomfortable.

"Man, that just won't do!" Cory screamed, trying to get their attention.

"But what can we do?" Ufei shrugged her shoulders.

Cory thought for a minute. Good question. What could they do?

"There must be something we can figure out. If I help you, then you can help me get to where I need to go to find more portal devices, ok?"

When no one responded, Cory asked, "What does the tunnel network look like? Do you have any type of map of the whole thing? And do you have anything on the layout of the town itself?"

Ufei nodded. "My father made it a priority to map everything under the city and as much of the city above as we could."

"Where are they? Can I see them?"

Tyncil looked at Ufei for the okay, and she gave a small nod. "We'll take you to the planning room," he said.

"Let's go then."

Cory wheeled to the entrance of the room and waited for one of them to begin pushing him. Tyncil came up behind him and Ufei stepped beside. "It's not far from here," she said.

"I'm all yours." Cory leaned back and folded his arms as Tyncil began pushing him out the door and through the tunnels.

With Ufei walking beside him, they wound through a short series of tunnels. Cory glanced behind and noticed none of the other Garlians were following.

"How come they're not coming?"

"They have other duties. Among them, waiting for the rescue party's return," Tyncil said.

Cory nodded as they wheeled him into a larger chamber that was very well lit. The walls were all stark white, and a center console, about ten feet long and three feet wide, stood as tall as the Garlians' waists. It reminded Cory of the puzzle table with the switches that he and Trevor had beaten to stop the wind and sound. But this one was as starkly white as the walls and it looked as if it was made of semi-opaque glass.

"Ok so, where are the maps?"

Tyncil stepped to the console, and like a master playing piano, his fingers danced over the surface, projecting a detailed schematic on the opposite wall.

"Wow, that's impressive. You guys still have some amazing technology left over from before, huh? The part of your world I've spent most of my time in was not like this at all." Cory studied the map display of the tunnel labyrinth and shook his head. "Can I see the town first?"

Tyncil nodded and after some more rhythmic conducting with his fingers over the console, a map of the town replaced the tunnels.

Cory studied it for a moment. "What do the blue squares represent?"

"Blue?" Ufei said.

"The same color as your coats."

Tyncil again looked at Ufei before answering. "Those are —"

"Wait!" Cory waved his arms. "If I'm going to try to help you, you can't keep things from me. So can you stop being so secretive, please?"

Ufei nodded. "Those are entrances from underground to the city above," Tyncil continued. "The blue means that they're still secret."

"As far as we know," Ufei corrected.

Tyncil continued his mastery of the console. Several triangles on the map lit up. "This color ..."

"Green," Cory supplied.

"Green. These are entrances from above that we know for sure have been discovered."

Cory nodded then wheeled himself around the console and up to the wall. "It's probably easier if I point."

He wheeled to the far edge of the map and pointed to three different brown circles. "What are these? And the other brown circles on the outskirts of the town?"

"Those are entrances to the tunnels on the outskirts of the town," Ufei began, then added, "I brought you down here through one of them. We've been able to keep them all secret so far."

"What are these large squares with thin outlines? There must be a dozen or more of them drawn in the town." Cory tapped a few of the squares for emphasis.

"Those are slave living-quarters," Tyncil said.

"There are some slaves in private homes too," Ufei added. "We can't do much about them unfortunately, but most who are taken become communal slaves who work in the town and live in those shared barracks."

Cory wheeled around the console and turned to see the wall from a distance again. "Ok, can I see the tunnel map again?"

Tyncil complied.

Again Cory asked question after question about its symbols, and Ufei and Tyncil did their best to answer. Finally Cory shook his head.

"At the moment, I don't see what you guys can do differently. It makes no sense whatsoever to keep sacrificing Garlians to rescue others. There must be a better way to help them escape and still protect your home here in the tunnels."

Cory continued to inspect the wall while Ufei and Tyncil kept quiet.

"What are those short, thick lines in the middle of some of the tunnels?" Cory wheeled back to the wall and pointed to several of the small marks he was referring to.

"Those are doors," Tyncil explained.

"Doors? I've never seen any doors in the tunnels," Cory said, turning from the wall to face the two Garlians.

Ufei glanced at Tyncil. "The doors are recessed into the sides of the tunnels," she said. "They're almost invisible."

"What are they for?"

Ufei shrugged. "We don't know what they were for."

"Do they still work?"

"We assume they do, but we've never used them. Having closed doorways would be dangerous when we're escaping in the dark."

Cory wheeled back and stopped next to the two Garlians. "Do those in the city know how to control them?"

Ufei frowned. "No, they don't know where the mechanisms are that open them."

"But you guys do?"

Tyncil nodded. "They're right there." He pointed to several small spiral symbols on the edges of the tunnels that corresponded to the fat, short lines representing the doors.

Cory slapped his knee. "There's your answer."

Ufei and Tyncil looked at each other, not understanding.

"What do you mean?" Tyncil asked.

 It's so simple!" Cory was nearly shouting. "You just need to plan your rescues more carefully so that your route back takes you past one of the doors early in the path. Close that door after you pass it but before your pursuers have, and you'll have the time to get away without one of you needing to sacrifice yourself. Even if the door is opened within a few minutes, it should give you more time than you'd ordinarily have by creating a diversion and getting someone captured. I can't believe none of you have thought of it before this."

"Danny, you were quiet back there." Christy tapped on his shoulder and signed when he turned to look at her.

Danny smiled. "In case you can't tell," he signed, "coming back wasn't my idea, but Brad wouldn't come without me."

Christy hugged her young friend. "I know," she said. "Thank you."

The group was standing in a room that looked familiar, though they knew it was in a city they'd never been in before.

Christy was thinking of what she'd heard as they were being whisked to this new location by the portal in Zyltruubanik.

"Did anyone hear Tarynn as the portal was about to start up?"

Nods from everyone but Brad and Danny confirmed what she'd heard.

"What do you think it meant?"

Detective Lockhart answered. "I don't know but I bet we're going to find out real soon. My guess is that name she said, 'Darynn,' is the counterpart to Tarynn and Sarynn."

"Ooh! Send that man to the head of the class," Darynn said, materializing.

Jack stepped forward toward the holographic girl. "Can you tell us where Cory went?" he asked.

Darynn frowned. "Cory?"

"Yeah, the kid in the wheelchair," Jack replied with a hint of annoyance in his voice. "Tarynn said he'd come here."

Darynn frowned again then stood still, her eyes taking on a glassy stare as she said in a very monotone voice, unlike the one she'd just used to address them, "You might have mentioned that." She clearly wasn't talking to anyone in the group.

Jack waited until Darynn's eyes again focused on them. "Who were you just talking with?"

"That imbecile, Tarynn. But no matter. So let's see, you want to find Cory. I can bring him here if you'll wait a bit. I'll be back."

In an instant, she was gone again.

Christy clapped her hands together for attention as everyone began to talk at once. "Listen, I don't think she's telling us the truth."

"Why's that?" her dad asked.

Christy looked at Brad and said as calmly as she could, "Brad, did you see the same thing with Darynn as you did with Tarynn?"

Brad lifted his eyes and nodded almost imperceptibly before shifting his gaze back down to his feet.

"Brad saw fluctuations of color around Tarynn and now Darynn. He says it's because they're lying. Cory isn't here."

"That sort of makes what we heard when we were beginning to port here sound a little sinister, doesn't it?" Jack said.

Brad began to walk around, gazing at the ceiling. He then stepped out of the room and headed off.

"I have to follow him," Danny said, bolting out the door after Brad.

Christy started for the door. "We should all follow. Something tells me this is one of those times where only Brad gets what's going on." As she left the room, she turned around to see some questioning stares. "Come on, hurry up."

"You heard the lady," Jack said.

CHAPTER 6

"**Y**ou can do this without sacrificing anyone," Cory said again. Ufei and Tyncil were both shaking their heads in disbelief.

Cory threw up his hands. "Ok, put up the map of Boakly again."

When Tyncil complied, Cory wheeled in front of the wall again and pointed. "Let's pick this slave quarters as an example. Now, if you were going to rescue someone from it, what route would you take back to here?"

Tyncil's fingers flew over the console and the schematic of the tunnels appeared. Ufei joined Cory at the wall.

"This entrance is how we'd get to that slave quarters," she said, running her finger over the closest blue square then tracing along one of the connecting tunnels. "These tunnels are all unlit unless we light them. But here," she said, side-stepping to her right to follow the tunnel with her finger, "is how we'd run the tunnels to return." She tapped a large grey square. "That is where we are now."

Cory reached up and pointed. "You passed two of the hidden doors along that route."

Just then, one of the Garlians who hadn't followed them to the planning room rushed in and whispered something to Ufei.

Ufei motioned Tyncil over and spoke to him in a whisper. He nodded and flew out of the room followed by the other Garlian.

"Didn't we just agree on no secrets? What was that all about?" Cory asked, exasperated.

"I'm sorry, this has nothing to do with you or our methods of rescuing our own," Ufei began, "but I suppose it can't hurt to tell you what's going on."

"Ok, I'm listening."

"We've been infiltrated by something that we fear greatly. Somehow it came down into the tunnels from the exact entrance that I used to bring you from the surface. It has terrorized dozens of us and is making its way here, I'm told."

"It?" Cory asked. He smiled as it dawned on him. "Wait, it isn't about this big, is it?" Cory held up his hands two feet apart.

Ufei nodded.

"With a long tail?" Cory added.

"Tail?"

Cory leaned forward and pointed to his lower back. Then swept his hand back a couple of feet and kept it there. "Grows out of the backside ... about that long." Then he sat back.

Ufei nodded.

"Well, again you're wrong — it does concern me. You're not planning to harm him, are you?"

"Oh no." Ufei shook her head. "We do not dare antagonize it for fear it will grow to its real size and kill many of us."

"Grow? Never mind. Take me to him." Cory was still grinning as he wheeled around the console toward the doorway and waited.

Ufei stepped behind him and pushed him through the door into the tunnel.

"I don't know how Murray followed me here," Cory said, shaking his head. "But it'll be great to see him again."

Rushing through the unknown city following Brad, Christy was struck by how similar to Vahuuldyn it was. Dimly lit side streets bathed in a green glow passed by them one by one as the whole group chased Brad along a broad, just as dimly lit, main thoroughfare.

Christy's dad, running next to her, blurted out breathlessly, "Why's he looking at the ceiling and the tops of the buildings we pass?"

If she could have shrugged while running, she would have, but instead she said, "Don't know, but I'm sure it's for a reason because he hardly ever looks up."

Upon following Brad down a narrow alleyway, they found he had stopped fifty yards or so ahead.

Danny immediately tapped Brad for attention. "What do we do now, Brad?" he signed.

Christy could have hugged him again. Despite his fear and the fact he didn't want to be in the Empty World, Danny had slipped right into his former role with Brad when it was needed.

Brad signed a brief response, and Christy relayed it to everyone in a whisper.

"Quiet, we're being chased."

Nobody had moved or spoken for several minutes when they began to hear voices. As the voices grew louder, it became clear that they were speaking Ancient. After a few more tense minutes, the voices merged with footsteps pounding the street. Their pursuers ran past the side street they were on and the sound of feet running and voices yelling gradually lessened until it was quiet once more.

Christy tapped Brad, realizing that Danny didn't know they'd heard voices. "Did you understand any of what they said?" she signed.

After watching Christy's hands, Brad dropped his eyes to the street, but he said aloud, "Yes."

"Brad, please, what did they say?" Christy asked.

"We can't miss this chance for more slaves."

Jack, who understood Ancient well, spoke up.

"Impressive. So Brad, you understand Ancient, sign language, and the Cleaner language?" He turned to Christy when Brad didn't say anything. "Can we talk out loud?"

"Brad?" Christy touched his sleeve.

Brad nodded. "Cory's not here," he said. "Darynn lied."

Doug stepped closer to Brad and asked him why he kept looking at the ceiling.

Brad kept his eyes on the street and didn't respond.

Christy was about to prompt him when Danny stopped her. He touched Brad like Christy had and signed rapidly. Brad responded and they went back and forth, their hands moving too rapidly for anyone else to follow.

Christy grinned. "It's so nice having Danny here," she said while the two were signing. "He can get so much more out of Brad than I can."

Danny finished signing with a flourish and turned to the rest of the group. "Darynn is a part of the computer system here. To project the image of herself and to talk she needs the projectors, and to see things she needs the cameras set up all over the city."

Jack chuckled and interrupted. "They must be mounted up high, on the buildings, right?"

Danny smiled. "Yes, and there aren't any in this alley, so we're invisible to her. And as you've heard, there are Ancients that want to make us slaves."

Doug grunted. "That's what Tarynn was referring to when she said we were all hers. She must have been talking to Darynn."

"But this city seems deserted," Mike Lockhart pointed out. "Where did the Ancients come from?"

Danny tapped Brad and they signed back and forth.

Danny frowned when they were done. "Bad news. Brad's not clear. He thinks most of the city is still deserted and that only a small section is inhabited by Ancients. They need slaves to fix up other sections so they can expand into them. Darynn sees the whole city except where there are no projectors and cameras. He says we'll never get out of here because there aren't enough areas blind to Darynn. No matter what direction we travel, she'll see us eventually."

Mike stopped Danny with a gesture and, making sure the boy would be able to read his lips, he asked, "How close are we to an exit out of the city? Does Brad know?"

Danny was about to sign when Brad startled them all by answering without any prompting.

"I know where the exit is. Cory's not here."

Mike cleared his throat. "I'll draw their attention away from everyone. Brad can tell me which direction I should head while you make a run for the exit."

Jack shook his head. "No, we stick together."

Mike waved him off. "Brad? You said we can't make it out, but if I occupy the Ancients and Darynn, can you lead everyone else out?"

Before Brad could answer, Doug spoke up. "You shouldn't do this alone. I'll help you. Together we make a more convincing group."

Brad looked up, making eye contact with Mike before dropping his gaze again.

"That's a yes," Christy said. She began sobbing.

Danny yanked Brad's sleeve and the two signed back and forth. Finally, Brad shook his head.

"No!" Danny groaned.

Only Doug hadn't understood the signing. Christy knew she didn't have to explain, but she did anyway.

"Brad says there's no other way."

Cory let Ufei push him through the darkened tunnels. When they came to a well-lighted section, Ufei slowed down almost to a crawl.

"What's wrong?" Cory asked.

Ufei stopped completely and took a deep breath. "Around the bend is the Kuueegar."

Cory began to laugh softly. "Kuueegar? Nice name," he scoffed. "Are we alone? Did the ones who first saw Murray leave?"

"Murray?"

"The Kuueegar. That's his name."

"Everyone has fled except a few still singing. I think that's your word for it."

Cory frowned. "I don't hear anything, so singing probably isn't what they're doing, but let's go forward and see."

Ufei took another deep breath and pushed until they rounded the bend. Immediately, Cory spotted Murray. The cat meowed and leaped up, scattering a half dozen Garlians prone on the tunnel floor. Murray raced through the path the Garlians had cleared as they pushed up against the walls away from him. He began purring even before he sprang onto Cory's lap.

"Hey pal, good to see you. How did you find me, I wonder." Cory scratched under his chin as Murray made himself right at home, circling and plopping down as if he'd never been gone. "I've seen some of your people in Vahuuldyn react this way to Murray as well. What's so special about him?" Cory considered also explaining the incident that had occurred when Trevor and Christy were attacked by Garlians in Vahuuldyn, and how they were scared off by Murray, but then thought better of it. When Ufei didn't respond to his question, he turned his head around to say something directly to her, but she had backed up and was now standing ten feet away.

"Really? Get back here. The cat isn't going to bite you or curse you or whatever it is you're afraid of."

When Ufei took a few tentative steps forward, Cory turned back to look at the Garlians who'd scattered and were now staring and pointing at the cat. Some were mouthing words but no sound was coming out. One of them was Tyncil.

Cory shook his head and spun his chair around to face Ufei, who immediately stopped her slow advance.

"What is it about this Kuueegar that is so frightening to you all?"

"It is the embodiment of all that is evil. At one time we were hunted almost to extinction by the Kuueegar."

"One tiny cat?" Cory asked.

"No, the Kuueegar is not the name for just one individual, but for the whole species."

"But I don't understand how a small cat can hurt you. It can't grow."

Ufei was shaking her head in disagreement. "Yes it can. These tunnels and all the cities of this world were once inhabited by roving packs of them. Huge monsters they were. And they fed on us. We could not outrun them nor kill enough of them to make a difference."

"Kuueegar," Cory said, rolling the word off his tongue. "When did this preying on you start?"

"Long ago. Nobody for the last ten generations has seen the Kuueegar. But we remember and are afraid when we see the little ones such as Murray."

Cory laughed. "Well, Murray can't grow. He's a different breed of cat. He's as big as he's going to get," he said. "But if all you Garlians believe what you just told me, it may come in handy."

◇ ◇ ◇

"There's no other way and Mike shouldn't do it alone, honey." Doug was hugging Christy, trying to console her. After a few more seconds, he gently pushed her away and turned to Jack. "And in case you were thinking of volunteering, you're needed here to stay with the kids a lot more than I am."

"There's got to be another idea," Christy said, still sobbing.

Jack put his arm around her shoulder. "You're the one who told us to trust Brad's judgment. Already he's figured out the setup of how the computer tracks everything in the city. So without him, we'd be captured already by Ancients, and we wouldn't even understand why or how."

Nobody said anything for almost a minute when Danny and Brad began signing. Brad also made gestures, pointing off in one direction and nodding.

Danny turned to Mike and Doug.

"Brad says to head that way," he said, pointing to mirror what Brad had just done. "We're going to follow Brad in the opposite direction after you two start and we hear you being chased. If we get no interference, Brad says we should hit the stairs to the outside in only a few minutes. Luring any Ancients away from us is important or we won't make it. He also says that your best chance to avoid being captured is to look up."

Mike chuckled. "Assuming we can see the cameras while running for our lives."

"Brad did," Christy stated.

"I can see why you argued for Brad to come back," Doug said, looking at his daughter. He patted Brad on the back, but Brad pulled away quickly from the physical contact, hunching his shoulders and covering his head with his hands.

"Sorry, Brad," Doug said, looking at Christy in surprise. He wasn't as familiar with Brad's aversion to touch as the others were, Christy knew. She and Danny used touch to get Brad's attention or to prompt some other outcome from him. It was a fine balance that the two of them had, if not mastered, then at least learned to use to everyone's benefit.

She frowned. Her dad wouldn't get the chance to learn more of Brad's ways because the group was about to split up and her dad and the detective wouldn't be heading out of the city with the rest of them.

"Ok, let's get this show on the road," Mike said.

Christy hugged her dad again. "This isn't fair."

"I think poor Trevor said something similar," Doug replied, tearing up right along with Christy. He again gently pushed her back.

"I love you," he said, but he was choked up to the point where his words were almost unintelligible.

"I love you too," Christy sobbed back, then stepped over to Mike, hugging him quickly. The others, except Brad, shook the two men's hands or clapped them on the back with murmurs of 'Good luck.'

After final nods to everyone, the two men stepped out of the alleyway and ran off in the direction Brad had pointed to.

Christy stood with the others and listened as her dad's and the detective's footsteps got fainter and then faded completely. Shouts off in the distance, and more pounding steps told the group that their plan had gotten results.

Without warning, Brad started at a run and turned in the opposite direction of where Mike and Doug had gone.

As the others scrambled to follow, Jack said, "He doesn't give much warning, does he?"

Chapter 7

"It has been too long a time to have heard nothing of the rescue party," Tyncil said, getting up from the tunnel floor and warily approaching Cory and the cat.

Ufei nodded. "We must assume they've all been captured, or worse."

Cory interrupted. "Do you have weapons?"

Ufei shook her head. "We don't believe in weapons. We have none to speak of, anywhere."

Cory's eyes widened. "Great! What's the word I'm looking for?" After a moment, it struck him. "Pacifists, that's it. I've landed in the middle of a bunch of pacifists. Not only that," he said, talking to Murray in his lap, "I'm trying to teach them how to spring their captured friends without using any weapons!"

He turned and looked at Ufei. "We would never allow weapons for any reason," she admitted.

"Of course you wouldn't." Cory threw his hands in the air. "Unbelievable! And the people in the city?"

Tyncil looked at Ufei then back at Cory. "They are warlike, yes. They have spears and knives."

Cory shook his head. "Funny, I haven't seen any weapons other than primitive ones in the Empty World, yet you have crystal power everywhere. But I suppose primitive is a break for you guys since you won't even use that."

Cory patted Murray again and turned to Ufei. "Can we go back to the maps? Let's plan a strategy to free your brother and that failed rescue party."

Ufei nodded. "I'll pick the rescue party after we plan."

Cory nodded. "You can pick who goes, but I'll do the rest of the planning." He wheeled around facing the way back to the planning room and gestured for Tyncil to push him.

As they were traveling back, Cory asked Ufei, "How come you're all young, no adults?"

"We are better at entering the city and freeing slaves. Once we reach adulthood we'll stop being part of the rescue parties," Ufei explained. "And the rescue parties keep separated from the elders and families with young ones in case we slip up and are followed back here. That way we won't give away the location of our homes, only where the rescue parties reside."

"Well, at least that makes sense," Cory said.

Back in the planning room, Cory had Tyncil put the schematic of the tunnels back up so he could study it as they waited for others who would form the rescue party to join them. When the others arrived, he wheeled himself up to the wall and traced a path. "Here's where you'll enter the tunnels after you rescue Abei and the others. I would use the closest door to where you enter," Cory said, pointing to the closest mark that represented a door, "instead of waiting for this one." He wheeled a few feet over and pointed to a door farther along. "That way you'll have this second one to fall back on if need be."

Ufei took control then, pointing out who she wanted to accompany her and Tyncil on the rescue mission.

"Whoa! Hold on there!" Cory interrupted. "Ufei, you stay back. I'll need you to close that door and then push me back with you. You and I are going to wait by that door while Tyncil and the rest of the rescue party enter the city and free your brother and the others. When they get back, we'll close that door behind them so they can't be followed."

A Garlian who had been selected to be part of the rescue party spoke up then, looking directly at Ufei.

"Why is the human making you push him? He's slowing you down."

Cory answered. He'd expected there to be comments and was ready for them.

"You haven't exactly had good results so far, have you? There will be plenty of time for Ufei to bring me back once she closes the door. And unless everyone has been going slow deliberately when we've raced through the tunnels, she's been more than able to keep up with you all so far while pushing me."

Nods of approval outnumbered the disbelieving stares, but Cory felt compelled to address the terrified looks that Murray was getting.

"He's not going to hurt you or eat you. He can't grow any bigger, ok?"

The stares of disbelief were mingled with outright fear. Cory shook his head, ready to give up the attempt to convince them, when Ufei stepped over.

She looked him right in the eyes for a second, then reached down and gave Murray a pat. There were some sharp intakes of breath from the startled group of Garlians. Murray started to purr and Ufei reached her other hand down and picked him up, cradling him on her shoulder.

"See?" she said, smiling. "He's harmless."

"Can we please wait a minute?" Christy pleaded. They had stopped to catch a collective breath at the bottom of the long stairway that led out of the underground city.

"That's not a good idea," Jack said. "We shouldn't waste any time."

Brad started up the steps at a run and took any chance for discussion or choice away from them. Jack and Danny followed immediately. Christy looked briefly back toward where they'd come from, stomped her foot, and then reluctantly hurried to keep up.

"This isn't what I expected," Jack said as they stepped into the open air. There was virtually no wind, and the dangerous sound they were so accustomed to were also absent.

Danny groaned and slid to the ground, exhausted from the climb, and Brad followed suit. Christy, however, didn't even notice the lack of wind or sound, or join the two slumped over. She just turned her back for some privacy and sobbed. Jack came up behind her, spun her around and wrapped his arms around her, pulling her close.

"I'm sorry, honey."

"I hate this world. I wish you and grandma had never discovered it. I've caused nothing but trouble for everyone since grandma left me the secret to this awful place."

Jack kissed the top of her head. "I wish I'd never found it either. Or really what I wish is that I could have had more time with your grandmother to discuss what we were going to do about it. Who we were going to share the secret with. She shouldn't have burdened you with this. I understand that she thought I was lost forever and had nobody to confide in, but it was so unfair to you."

"No, grandpa, she did the right thing. I screwed it all up. She told me in the letter to think carefully before I did anything. To think about the consequences of whatever actions I took. I just didn't do that. I couldn't wait to see for myself, and that started this whole mess. It's been well over a year and Rob's hearing is still not back. It's probably gone for good. And Cory will never walk again. Your best friend in this world, Clacker, is dead. I know you tell me it's you and grandma's fault but really if I'd been more careful like she'd asked, none of this would have happened."

Danny stood up and walked over to Christy, tugging on her sleeve to get her attention. She separated herself from her grandfather's hug and looked expectantly at her friend.

"Christy, stop it. I read your lips. You aren't to blame for any of this. We've argued this out before. I don't feel sorry for Cory at all. He brought everything on himself. He pushed Rob into the pond. He tried to untie the glider and broke his back falling. And because he planned with Brad to come here then threatened to leave him behind, Brad made his own decision, which caused me to follow him."

Danny paced back and forth, getting more agitated as he was recounting events. "I'm here now only because you need Brad and he wouldn't come back without me." He crossed his arms defiantly. "So I don't want to hear you blame yourself again, you got that?"

Through her sobs, Christy smiled and reached out to Danny, hugging him. She knew she needed the hug more than Danny. He was the youngest of them all but he'd proven time and time again to be the one who could keep it together no matter what they were facing. She hugged him tighter.

Jack clapped his hands for attention. "Alright, we have to go. No telling if or when someone will be following us." Jack reached down to offer a hand to Brad. When his gesture was ignored, he just repeated, "We have to go."

Christy let Danny out of the hug but grabbed hold of his hand. Danny stooped down to Brad's eye-level and motioned him up with his free hand. Promptly, Brad got up, eliciting an amazed look from Jack.

"Ok then, keep your eyes peeled. This landscape looks different from anything I've ever traveled through here before," Jack said, readjusting his pack.

Christy nodded. "It looks different to me too. I just noticed the wind and sound are missing."

"Remember, that doesn't mean we won't hit pockets of sound," Jack cautioned. "We could just be in a sound free stretch. We've traveled through a lot of these before, but they always lead to more sound areas."

Danny, who had been watching their lips, spoke up. "But where are we headed? How are we going to find Cory?"

Tyncil led the small rescue party. He and the two other members of the party had moved quickly ahead as Ufei pushed Cory toward where the recessed door was. They traveled in complete darkness and Cory marveled at how easily Ufei seemed to navigate; the rescue party had removed the crystals from any lighted section of the tunnels as they went, but it didn't seem to hinder them at all.

Finally they slowed to a stop. "We're here. Now we wait," Ufei said.

"How do you know we're here?" Cory asked, genuinely curious.

"I can see the whole tunnel in my head. Can't you?"

"In your head?"

Cory felt Ufei nodding. "We can see the tunnels in our heads almost like the maps we projected on the wall, but without details such as the location of doors. Putting the maps up was for your benefit. We wouldn't have needed them to plan a route back. The whole system of tunnels is always there in our heads as long as we've walked them at least once. We never get lost. As you've seen, our eyes are much smaller than yours and our eyesight is that much poorer. If it weren't for our navigational insight, we'd be helpless."

"So anyone chasing you wouldn't have that same advantage if they've never been down here before?"

"That is correct."

"But you're at the same disadvantage in the town?"

"Yes, but in daylight we can at least see the streets and alleys, even if we don't know where they lead. But we've been to all the areas that they hold slaves in, so we could navigate to them even at night. But the Boaklians don't yet have navigational insight, so that's to our advantage. Unless we've lighted a tunnel section or it's one that has been discovered by the Boaklians on their own, they can't follow instinctively."

Cory was surprised — not at their ability to navigate, because he'd seen that at work since he first met Ufei, but because he hadn't heard any of the Garlians call those who lived above 'Boaklians' before.

"Ufei?"

"Yes?"

"What do you call yourselves? For instance, I'm 'human.' A group of us would be called humans. What is your name for yourselves as a whole species?"

"Qylee."

Cory nodded in the dark. "Are the Boaklians Qylee?"

"Yes, of course. What else would they be unless they were human, like you?"

"So you've never heard of Ancients or Cleaners?"

"What are they?"

Cory shook his head. "I don't believe it. You haven't met any other intelligent species around here." He paused for a second before explaining. "They're two other intelligent species that live in this world. I don't know what you'd call them if you knew of them, but we call them Ancients and Cleaners."

Ufei was silent for several seconds. "That's not possible. We are the only ones."

Cory chuckled to himself. "Oh yeah, Ufei? I'm not Qylee, yet I'm here. And you've known about humans for years. You learned our language from one of us a long time ago. Believe me, you may not have met them, but there are two other intelligent species here."

Again Ufei took a long few seconds before she responded. "We will discuss this further after our rescue mission is complete."

For the rest of their mission, they waited in silence. Cory had run out of questions, and Ufei did not seem to be in the talking mood. After what Cory assumed must have been an hour or more, they began to hear sounds drifting toward them. As the sounds got closer, they resolved into footsteps echoing off the walls — footsteps pounding rapidly and growing louder by the second.

"Get ready," Ufei warned, the tension evident in her voice.

Suddenly a clatter of noise was upon them. Rustling clothes and footsteps brushed past. Cory felt the stirring of the wind as bodies passed them at a run. The last person grunted something in Garlian, and Ufei sprang into action. She let go of Cory's chair and the sound of her steps receded for a second. A grinding sound met his ears and a momentary snap, and suddenly his chair was grabbed, and they were on the run, following the rescue party.

"It got stuck." Ufei blurted out after they'd turned a sharp bend in the tunnel.

"What? It's still open?"

"Yes."

"Stop at the next one then. Plan B."

What was only three minutes or so later, Ufei stopped the wheelchair. Cory heard her retreat back a few yards and then heard that grinding sound again. It went on for a second longer than the last one but it too ended with a sickly snapping sound.

Cory felt Ufei as she came back and rested her hands on the wheelchair handles.

"It's stuck also." The disappointment was thick in Ufei's voice. "Hopefully I can create a diversion enough to give the others the time needed to escape. I'm sorry, you'll be caught too." She turned his chair around again to face where their pursuers would be coming from.

Cory was nervously stroking Murray's back. Murray had been calm for the duration of their long runs in the dark.

"Ufei? Are you near a crystal slot to light this section?"

"Yes, why?"

"Light this stretch and then follow your rescue party without me. I have an idea. Go. I'll slow them down and hopefully join you later."

"Even if you could get away, you don't know how to get back to us."

The reality of her statement deflated the excitement building in Cory but he said, "Go, just do it. I'll find a way."

Ufei seemed about to argue but the sounds of pursuit were coming closer, echoing off the walls.

"Good fortune shine on you," she said as she let go of his chair. Within a few seconds, light flooded the tunnel.

Cory squinted from the brightness as he spun his chair around, searching for the girl. He found Ufei in a second. She was twenty yards away, staring at him.

"Go!" he screamed.

Ufei nodded a goodbye salute, then turned and disappeared around the next bend in the tunnel.

CHAPTER 8

"**D**anny brings up a great point. Where *do* we go?" Jack said. They were grouped together at the top of the stairs out of Abuuenki, and had no plan for where to go next.

"Brad?" Christy said, gently. "Do you have any ideas?"

Brad ignored her, his head down as he stood slightly apart from the other three. Danny took a step towards him and touched his sleeve. Seeing that Brad was focused on his hands, he started to sign quickly. Brad watched without any emotion, but replied in rapid, short bursts of signing, intermingled with a couple of nods and pointing off in the distance.

Danny took a deep breath, looked confused, then before explaining what Brad had signed, he qualified it by saying, "I don't understand completely why or how he knows what he just said but here it goes. Cory was not sent out of the city of Zyltruubanik through the portal to Abuuenki like we were."

"Wait," Jack interrupted. "How does he know Cory wasn't still in the city?"

Danny got Brad's attention and signed a short burst.

To everyone's surprise, Brad answered verbally.

"Not lying."

Jack quickly responded. "Nobody's saying you're lying, Brad."

Brad spun around and started grunting out of frustration as he covered his face with his hands and stomped his feet.

Jack looked as if he was going to say something else, but Christy tapped his arm and shook her head at him. "Jack didn't understand, did he, Brad? You meant that Tarynn wasn't lying when she said Cory had left, didn't you? When Tarynn said Cory left the city, she didn't change color like she did when you think she lied to us. Is that it?"

Brad didn't respond but he stopped grunting and turned around, facing everyone, though he still gazed at the ground.

"Sorry Brad," Christy apologized. "Go ahead, Danny, tell us what else Brad said."

Danny was frowning, trying to understand. "So that's how Brad knows Cory was sent out of the city. He didn't go through the portal like we did — that was a lie. But it wasn't a lie when Tarynn said Cory left the city, so he must have gotten out of the underground to the surface. There must be some other way than steps to get out."

After a pause, Jack interrupted. "I'm sorry I misunderstood what you meant, Brad. I'm glad that Christy knew," he said. "And Danny, what you're saying all makes sense. Keep going."

Danny nodded. "Brad says we need to go there." He pointed just like Brad had. "He's afraid Cory may be lost out here somewhere."

"But where? How do we know where to go, what direction to head in?"

"Cory needs me." Brad started repeating to himself.

Danny beckoned Christy with his hand. "Let me see the pictures you took. We should be able to figure out where we need to go, I hope."

Christy pulled out her camera and after turning it on, scrolled through the photos and then handed it to Danny.

Danny looked at the photo of the mural, and touching the screen, expanded it to zero-in on one region. He pointed, turning the screen to show Brad. "Brad, we know that this is Zyltruubanik. We were sent to Abuuenki. It looks like it's a long way between the two. But if we go the way you want us to, it will get us back to Zyltruubanik, right?"

Brad stood there, not making eye contact but nodding his head slightly.

Danny smiled. "I guess we're headed in the right direction. Maybe we'll find Cory as we get closer. I wonder how he's going to get around outside?"

"That's a good question," Jack said.

Brad reached toward Danny, clearly asking for the camera. Danny handed it over with a puzzled look on his face.

Once Brad had the camera in his hands, he placed his thumb and index finger on the screen and spread them apart, enlarging the photo on the screen even further and then shifting it to show what he wanted. "Cory can move on that."

Christy and Danny crowded around him with Jack peeking over their shoulders.

"What's that?" Christy asked soothingly, hoping to get Brad to expand on what he was showing them.

When Brad didn't say anything, Danny took it and looked closer. "Is that some kind of tramway?"

"I think you're right, Danny. That's what it looks like," Jack said, rubbing his chin in thought. "That complicates things if he can get around. At least, it certainly doesn't make things easier."

"But if he's headed this way?" Christy offered. "Maybe it's a good thing. We might find him a lot sooner than we would if he wasn't."

"Could be." Jack shrugged. "Let's get moving, we have a long way to go no matter what. And we still may be followed if ...." He didn't finish the sentence.

Christy let out a sob, realizing her grandfather was going to mention the detective and her dad's part. If something on their end got messed up, the rest of them could still be in danger of being hunted.

"Don't worry, honey. Your dad and Mike are going to be ok. I promise when we find Cory, I'll come back and get them out any way I can. And it's possible that they can avoid capture. Who knows!"

Christy held back tears. "You're right," she said. "We have to go now, or what they're doing could be for nothing."

Cory sat in the path, listening as the pursuers got closer. He nervously stroked Murray's back, hoping the cat would make all the difference in whatever inevitable confrontation lay ahead.

"Whoa, careful, Murray." Just as three, then a fourth, then a fifth Garlian came into view, Murray sprang up and arched his back, hissing. The Garlians stopped ten feet way; all five of them had spears in their hands and knives tucked in black belts they wore around their waists. Instead of the usual blue shimmering coats that Cory was used to seeing, these Garlians had tan shirts and what looked almost like sweatpants, stained and in tatters.

Just like the Garlians that Murray had scared off when Cory had come upon Trevor and Christy being attacked, these Garlians began a high pitched sing-song chant and dropped down to their knees, bending forward till their foreheads touched the tunnel floor.

Cory wheeled himself a few feet closer and the Garlian farthest away got up and scurried back out of view. Cory could still hear him babbling something. The closest Garlian hadn't even lifted his head when his companion bolted, but one of the other ones did. He too began shouting something, and turned back toward where the other had run. Some type of angry exchange happened between them, and the other three stopped their chanting.

The Garlian closest to Cory lifted his head finally and stared right in Cory's eyes, then nervously shifted his gaze to Murray. The other two lifted their heads and stared too. The one who'd had the angry exchange with the deserter finally turned and joined his companions in staring.

Cory gripped his wheels tighter and inched closer again. This time, the remaining four screamed in unison and leapt up, disappearing down the tunnel.

"Well, Murray, it seems you saved my bacon. Those spears looked nasty." He spun around to follow Ufei and the rescue party when he heard a shout behind him.

Traveling rapidly once they'd escaped out of Abuuenki, Christy, Jack, and Danny were on high alert, looking for any signs of pursuit from the Ancients in the city. None of them were in any mood to talk, so they walked in silence. Brad walked beside Danny and seemed fascinated with the surrounding scenery, constantly turning from side to side, peering at each new thing. He even stooped down to pick up a flowering plant and Danny had to gently coax him to get up and keep moving.

After an hour at a frantic pace that left them all gasping for breath, they eased up a bit and began to converse with one another.

"This is so different," Christy said.

Jack nodded, understanding exactly what she meant. "I know, this looks much more like Earth. There's been almost no moss. And the grasses and other plants don't look as if they've adapted to wind." He pointed ahead to a dark patch of dense trees rising like a sinister barrier in the distance. "And it looks like we're headed into a real forest. That will be a first for me here."

As soon as Jack finished his comments, Brad stopped in his tracks, shaking his head.

Christy frowned. "What's the matter, Brad?"

Keeping his eyes glued to the ground, Brad extended his hand, clearly expecting someone to give him something.

Danny stepped in front of Brad and signed in his line of sight. "What do you want?"

Brad signed a reply and then started running back in the direction they'd come from, leaving the others startled.

"Brad, stop! Wait up!" Christy shouted as she took off after him, Jack and Danny following right behind.

After a hundred yards or so, Brad stopped abruptly, causing Christy to stumble into him. They both tumbled to the ground.

Jack caught up and reached a hand down to Christy, pulling her up. He offered the same to Brad who just ignored it and stood up on his own. Danny joined them, huffing from the short burst of running.

"The camera, that's what Brad asked for," Danny wheezed, out of breath. Brad just stood there, staring at his own feet again.

Christy took the camera out, and putting it in Brad's line of sight, she said, "Here it is."

Brad nodded, took the camera and expertly turned it on, scrolled through the photos on the back screen, expanded one to enlarge a section, and handed it back to Christy.

Christy frowned, showing it to Jack and Danny. Danny looked puzzled then snapped his fingers. "That must be a representation of a forest. Look, those could be tree symbols. They're not too different than we use for tree symbols on a map. Is that the forest we're heading to, Brad?"

Brad shook his head violently. "No, we can't go there. Go around."

Jack took the camera from Christy and looked at the expanded section of the photo. "Brad may have a point. I think he's seen something we missed." Jack pointed at a small symbol on the picture, dead center in the forest section. "Either a skull and crossbones is a universal symbol of danger across worlds, or humans had something to do with the mural. But in any case, that forest has a clear warning attached to it."

Cory was confronted by one of the Garlians who apparently was not as afraid of Murray as the others, and a spear was now pointed in Cory's direction.

The menacing Garlian crept toward him slowly. Even though fear showed on the Garlian's face, he kept coming closer.

Cory slipped his arm under Murray and lifted the cat up. Thankfully Murray took over, stretching and arching his back, and finally standing on Cory's lap.

That stopped the Garlian cold. A quiet sing-song chant came out of his mouth, seemingly without his lips even moving.

Cory got as close as he dared with the spear still pointing at him. "Back off, Buddy. Don't you know this cat will grow so large that he'll easily eat you?"

The Garlian confronting him turned his head and shouted behind. When there was no response, he tried it again, only much louder. Off in the distance, someone replied. The sound of that reply echoed toward them, and caused the Garlian's mouth to slant up in a vicious grin.

Whatever the Garlian's shout, and whatever the reply, it emboldened the Garlian, who took three more steps toward Cory and extended his spear, pressing it into Cory's shin. Cory was pretty certain that if Murray wasn't on his lap, the spear would be poking into his chest, not aimed downward into his shin,

More shouts from behind the Garlian echoed off the walls. The Garlian never took his eyes off Murray but he shouted some reply, all the while grinning with that venomous twist to his thin lips.

Within seconds, two Garlians came up behind their companion. The Garlian holding Cory stationary with his spear barked something. One of the other Garlians lowered his spear to a menacing level and stepped closer.

The third Garlian began chanting as he slipped past Cory and went a few feet behind. Cory felt that one's spear poke him in the back through his wheelchair.

The first Garlian slung his spear over his shoulder and motioned to Cory to follow him. With two spears still pointing at him, Cory knew it wasn't a request.

Cory started pushing his chair to follow the Garlian. The second Garlian remained facing Cory and kept his spear pointed at the wheelchair while walking backwards. Cory could still feel the spear tip of the third Garlian pressing into his back.

"Ok, Murray, we're in trouble now."

Chapter 9

"We shouldn't ignore Brad. If he thinks we should go around this forest, then we should," Danny said, signing and speaking aloud. Christy agreed.

Jack scratched his chin and looked at Brad; he was rocking from one foot to the other and mumbling to himself. "Ok, let's do it," Jack conceded.

"Danny, would you—" Christy started signing, but before she could say anything else, Brad took off at a brisk walk, following a new path.

As soon as the others caught up, Brad slowed down, slung his backpack off and pulled out his ear protection, slipping them on his head.

Danny tapped Christy on the sleeve. "Can I see your camera?" he signed.

She handed it over. Danny used the LCD screen to search for the mural again. Expanding a section, he smiled and pointed.

Christy and Jack leaned in.

"Everybody get your ear protection on. Those wavy lines are pretty obvious," Jack said, then looked at Brad and added, "How does he do that?"

They walked for a few more minutes when Jack tentatively lifted his ear protection up and motioned for Christy to do the same before saying, "I'm beginning to wonder ... are symbols really that universal? I guess the tree symbol and the sound symbol could be universal, but I can't reconcile the skull and crossbones. I can't imagine that being anything but human. How did those get on that mural if they're human in origin?"

Christy shrugged, saying nothing. Danny hadn't been watching Jack's lips, and Brad, who was slightly in the lead, didn't offer any response either. If he had, it would have surprised all of them equally.

They walked for another half an hour after slipping their ear protection back in place. They were following a crumbling road with weeds choking all available cracks. The pavement, although decayed, had flecks of sparkling minerals imbedded in it, which made it flash and dance as the light hit it. A few earthlike bushes and scrawny misshapen trees had managed to push through some of the larger cracks, adding to the eerie landscape.

Off to their right, the forest Brad had so vehemently wanted to avoid grew larger as they skirted around it.

Danny tugged on Christy's sleeve. Signing and nodding at Brad, he asked, "No sound yet?"

Christy lifted one ear cup slightly and shook her head.

Eventually the crumbling road they were on widened out to double its width, and off to each side broken walls and half buried foundations witnessed them passing. Brad seemed to have lost his fascination with the surrounding landscape, but the others found the new ruins interesting and walked slower, taking in the sights.

Cresting a small rise in the landscape, their eyes fell on a two story circular building with a massive diameter. It reminded Christy of a football stadium, but it was covered with what seemed like a thousand years of debris, and looked as forlorn as any of the crumbling walls and foundations they'd just passed.

The closer to it they got, the stranger it appeared. There were no windows that they could discern and it was a dull gray color, with patches of red streaks trailing down in random patterns. Reinforced ribs of the same color gray were spaced fifty yards apart along the walls. Jack waved them all to a halt in front of it and pointed high. "There's a tree sticking up through the roof ... or maybe the roof is missing completely."

Brad stepped off the road and headed toward the building, starting to walk around its perimeter. When he disappeared from sight, Christy waved them on to follow him.

They caught up to Brad and found him leaning his forehead on the side of the building.

Danny tugged on Christy's sleeve. "He removed his ear protection," he signed. Christy and Jack removed theirs also.

Jack frowned. Puzzled, he stepped to the wall and tapped on it. No sound issued forth. Jack tried again — same results.

"That's odd — it feels like metal but there's no echo when tapping it. It appears very thick too."

Danny waved to get everyone's attention. "Look," he spoke and signed. "It looks like it's partially buried."

Jack knelt down, examining where the building met the surrounding ground. Digging into the packed dirt up against the building with his hands, he began to uncover what looked like the top of a doorway. Standing and wiping his hands off against his pants, he said, "I think you're right, Danny. There's at least one whole story completely covered up"

"Brad's gone further around the building, come on," Christy urged.

Jack stood up and gestured to Danny, and they all followed Brad.

As they hurried around the massive building to catch up to Brad, the ground that had covered the lower part of the structure receded till they could see what looked like the beginnings of a foundation. The curve of the building hid Brad till they finally got close to him. He stood in front of an entrance. Jutting out twenty feet perpendicular from the building was a ten foot high, eight foot wide structure. A closed door was on the end. Brad was standing in front of the door, his hands flying over it in an indecipherable pattern. Suddenly, the door slid open and Brad disappeared inside.

"How'd he — ?" Jack began.

"Child's play," Christy answered, smiling as she stepped through the door.

The town of Boakly was even stranger close up than it had appeared from a short distance.

Construction appeared to have proceeded without rhyme or reason. Buildings were jutting out at odd angles and second and third stories rose up with swaying makeshift catwalks bridging them over the streets below. An occasional strip of indigo or yellow cloth hung from flagpoles sticking out of glassless windows and flapped in the light breeze, adding the only hint of color to the chaotic scene.

Despite the presence of Murray, or maybe because if it, the Garlians let Cory talk as they led him through Boakly's streets.

"This makes no sense, Murray. We rode in an elevator from the tunnels below to get here, so there's definitely power here, but I don't see any signs of its use in the town so far. Even the lights that I saw from a distance are just torches up close."

"And you won't." The sound of someone speaking in English startled Cory.

As the voice spoke, Cory's escort stopped abruptly and Cory spun around. Standing there was the oldest Garlian he had seen yet.

The Garlian was dressed all in black, with a short sleeved shirt and loose fitting pants both decorated with intricate crisscrossing silver thread. The man wore no shoes but had a tight fitting cap on his head. His exposed skin was visibly wrinkled and his eyes yellowish and clouded, not the clear black of the other Garlians.

With a wave of dismissal from the old Garlian, Cory's three escorts melted away into the shadows.

"English," Cory said, hoping to hide his growing fear. Had he met the Garlian who would send him to his death because, according to Ufei, there was no use for a person in a wheelchair? "I thought nobody in this town knew English."

"You have been misinformed. No doubt by that rabble who live like rats beneath us." The Garlian stepped closer and stopped a few feet from the wheelchair. His head tilted down toward Murray. "He won't help you. I know the truth of cats his size. It is nothing more than a housecat."

With the wary but not fearful responses Murray had received in the town so far, Cory wasn't surprised by this.

The old Garlian walked around the wheelchair slowly. "You are unable to walk."

Cory hesitated, then nodded, seeing no point in trying to say something to the contrary.

"It wasn't a question. I was not told you would be unable to walk."

Cory frowned. Despite his fear, the comment was odd. "Told?"

The Garlian ignored him and called out something in his own language. One of the three Garlians reappeared and the old Garlian seemed to issue some short commands before stepping in front of Cory and beginning to walk ahead. His chair moved as the other Garlian gripped the handles and pushed to keep up with the retreating figure.

"Where are you taking me?" Cory called out to the Garlian in front.

The old Garlian turned around. "I would not bother with you. But I was told to look out for any humans."

"Who told you to look out for humans?" Cory asked again.

The old Garlian ignored the question, turned around, and motioned for his companion to follow. Cory threw his hands up in frustration. All he could do was wait and see what was in store for him. But the fear came back stronger than ever, washing over him like a cold wave.

"We can't keep this up forever," Doug said. He was out of breath, already slumping to the floor. "Eventually, they'll catch on to what we're doing."

"Agreed. It's just a matter of time." Mike was leaning up against a wall, sucking air in large gulps.

"I think we've served our purpose and Brad has them out of here by now."

Mike nodded. "Then maybe we can find our way out of here too. If not, at least you're right, we did what we had to."

"Do you have any idea where we are in relation to the stairs out?"

Mike shook his head. He shrugged, smiling grimly. "I'm completely lost."

Doug inhaled and exhaled loudly, then calmed his breathing down. "Me too."

Mike closed his eyes, enjoying the rest. "Makes you realize how amazing Brad is, doesn't it?"

Doug closed his eyes too. "You know, his family has lived next door to us for years but I never saw him much. I think Abigail has kept him sheltered from everything by using Cory as a buffer. The fact that Brad figured out the portal devices, learned an alien language in minutes according to Christy, and identified how we can travel to safely avoid capture here, seems unbelievable. Not to mention he solved numerous locked doors almost instantaneously."

"You have to credit Danny and Christy for understanding how to approach talking and interacting with him," Mike added, agreeing. "Together they've made him more comfortable with us than I would have thought possible."

Doug chuckled, shaking his head.

Mike frowned. "What?"

"We've got a teenage girl who blames herself for all this, a preteen boy who's deaf, and an autistic teenage boy with amazing abilities. The three of them will get everyone through this. Not to mention we sent home a kid who has more courage than five of me combined." Doug was silent for a second. "I owe my life to Trevor."

Mike nodded again then stood away from the wall. "We better get going and do whatever it is we plan to do."

Doug opened his eyes and stood up. "What direction should we head?" He turned around to take a better look at the small alley they'd ducked into to avoid the Ancients. "I wonder if there's any way out without heading onto the main streets again."

"Worth a try. If we're lucky, there won't be any cameras the farther in we get." Mike slapped Doug on the shoulder as they started.

After a few minutes, the alley sloped downward and ended abruptly.

"Oh well," Mike groaned.

"I guess this means we head back into the main streets," Doug said, resigned to the dangerous task.

"I guess you're right."

Doug hesitated. He knew running through the main streets again, they would risk almost certain capture. "Hold on a minute, Mike. Let's try to think like Brad for a moment," he said, frowning at the seemingly impenetrable obstacle in front of them.

Mike shook his head. "That's impossible for either of us."

Doug shrugged. "Agreed, but what do we have to lose? Let's assume there is a door here; we just can't see yet. I think that's what he'd do."

"But it's a wall ..." Mike said.

Doug nodded, "You're right. But why does this alley just end abruptly? There has to be something here, some type of doorway. Nothing else makes sense."

Mike shrugged. "If I hadn't seen Brad in action, I'd feel foolish standing in front of a dead end hoping for a doorway." He pressed his face up to the smooth surface and began systematically running his eyes over it.

Doug stood back, glancing behind, worried that they'd shortly hear their pursuers heading towards them.

Whoa, what have we here?" Mike whispered. "It almost looks like some sort of outline. Doesn't it?" Mike traced the outline of a door with his hand.

"See? Already we've taken advantage of Brad's way of thinking without him being here." Doug grinned, turning back to see what Mike had found. .

"Yes, but we're not him. If it is a door, I can't see how to open it." Mike continued to run his hand over the outline.

"There has to be some sort of hidden mechanism somewhere," Doug said, turning and searching the adjoining walls.

"Any indentations or structural flaws?" Doug asked. He looked back toward Mike who was meticulously running his hands over the surface and shaking his head.

"Wait, I think I have something," Mike said suddenly. He was reaching up high along the top edge of the nearly invisible outline of the door. Sliding his hand along it, he began tapping. Suddenly his finger disappeared into a small hole, hidden by shadows and clever construction.

The doorway slid back, grinding and complaining all the way, but opening up completely.

"Well, I'll be." Mike grinned. "Who'd a thunked it?"

"Brad would have," Doug answered, grinning and slapping Mike on the shoulder as they both stepped through the open door.

CHAPTER 10

"This world is full of surprises," Jack said, barely above a whisper. The four of them stood overlooking the inside of the massive circular structure Brad had guided them into.

Upon entering, they'd moved along the short access corridor to the edge of an overlook that revealed the whole of the building to them. They were several stories above the floor with no visible way to get down to it, so they had nowhere to go from there. The building held nothing but years of decay and debris. Scraggly trees and weeds had taken root in the dirt floor.

Seeing it from the inside, it looked even more like a stadium than it had from the outside, except for the lack of seats. The floor below curved downward, creating a kind of bowl beneath them.

"It doesn't look like there ever was a roof. I wonder what this was," Christy said.

Brad turned around and walked back into the empty corridor they'd come down. He picked up a baseball sized chunk of the wall of the access corridor that had crumbled to the floor and came back to the others, who were still staring at the immense space in front of them.

"What are you doing, Brad?" Christy asked.

Brad pushed through the others and right up to the edge. Christy was about to caution him when he stopped and hurled the debris in his hand. It hit a particularly clean area of the floor below.

If Brad was expecting the result he got, he hadn't shown it ahead of time and the others were completely caught by surprise.

The second the chunk of broken wall hit the floor, the whole place seemed to come alive. An earsplitting boom rang out and the massive floor rippled, throwing dirt and small things up into the air.

The shockwave of air and sound rushed at them before they could do anything. They were thrown back several feet, all of them landing in a heap on the floor.

As the loose debris thrown up into the air fell back down, more booms rang out and more air rushed at them. While lying helplessly on the floor, all except Danny covered up their ears, waiting for the chain reaction of sound and wind to end.

Finally, after several minutes had passed, things quieted down.

Danny got up first. He'd been struck by the air like the others, but the sound hadn't affected him because he hadn't heard it.

"What happened?" he yelled, reaching down to help Christy. Jack slowly got up and helped Brad to his feet, the boy squirming out of his grasp quickly once he was up.

"What was that?" Danny asked, looking directly at Christy.

Christy shook her head. She signed and spoke to make sure Danny would understand her. "Danny, I can't hear you, my ears are ringing. I can't hear anything just now."

Jack waved for attention, then signed, "I can't hear anything either. There was a loud noise and blasts of air, Danny."

Danny nodded then turned to Brad. "Your ears too?" he signed.

Brad nodded almost imperceptibly. "I'm sorry," he signed back.

"Is everyone ok?" Jack asked, signing.

Danny gave the thumbs up and Christy nodded. Jack tapped Brad's arm and signed it again. Brad met his eyes for a split second.

Jack smiled. "Ok, then," he continued, signing. "I think we know how the Ancients generated that sound now and why we've not needed our ear protection in this area. This speaker, or whatever you want to call it, isn't working any longer. I think we should count ourselves lucky that there's so much debris and growth accumulated in here. If this was still clear of all that, the noise would probably have been much worse and destroyed our eardrums."

Christy turned to look out at the still slightly vibrating expanse. "That's some speaker," she signed.

"I hope we don't ever meet whatever generates the wind up close," Danny signed.

Back outside, Christy thought about what her grandfather had said and knew he was right. They'd been lucky. They could all easily have ended up like Rob: their hearing gone, damaged by the Empty World. She wondered how Rob was doing. Despite some early hope that his hearing would recover, it was now pretty clear it never would. Remembering the whole incident and how Danny had helped Rob cope, Christy reached over and squeezed Danny's arm. He looked at her questioningly. "What?" he signed.

She just smiled at him, shaking her head that it was nothing, and squeezed again.

As panic rose in him, all Cory could do was look at the ruined town they were traveling through. It wasn't much of a distraction. The withered old Garlian ahead continued to guide them to some undisclosed location.

Despite the situation, Murray was purring away contentedly. Cory patted him, nervously stroking the cat's back and scratching him under the chin.

After a twenty minute journey, the old Garlian stopped in front of an open doorway to a dilapidated wooden building. Barking out orders to the Garlian doing the pushing, the old Garlian pointed and Cory found himself being wheeled into the building, down a corridor, and into a room, until he was left there alone. On his way out, the Garlian pulled a rusted metal gate from a recess in the doorway and slid it across the opening, fastening it securely.

Cory exhaled loudly. He'd been holding his breath without realizing it. Wheeling around slowly, he explored the three dirty walls and the rusted but solid metal gate. The walls were made up of slats of wood that had, at some point in the distant past, been painted white, but now were a dingy gray flaking mess. The back wall opposite the gate had two large spots which had been covered by squares of even dirtier wood, presumably to cover holes. The place looked bad and smelled worse.

If I wasn't in this wheelchair, those rickety walls wouldn't hold me, he thought.

For the first time since his first week in the hospital after he broke his back, he felt overwhelming anger at the world.

For several minutes he wallowed in self-pity and cried. Then, unexpectedly, Murray stood up on his lap and stretched, nuzzling Cory's chin and purring loudly.

Cory's first reaction was to push Murray away, but Murray was persistent and Cory gave in, feeling bad that he'd reacted negatively to him. Wiping tears out of his eyes, he hugged the cat close to him and was rewarded with a lick of his face and even louder purring.

"Thanks Murray."

"Touching." The mocking voice of the old Garlian startled Cory. He wheeled around to face the metal gate and the menacing grin of the Garlian peeking through it.

"You know," Cory began, trying to build his own courage up by taunting the old Garlian, "It took at least ten of you guys to bring down one girl and one boy, both friends of mine." Cory frowned when he said that, wondering if the 'friend' part was accurate, but he continued anyway. "And as soon as Murray here came on the scene, you all scattered faster than a pile of leaves in a hurricane. Cowards, all of you."

The Garlian's eyes narrowed in anger. "There'll be no scattering around here. Your little pet— yes I know what you call those small creatures— can't scare me or those who serve me." The old Garlian turned to leave then turned back. "Oh, and just so you know ... you are my bait for the underground rabble. You may be here awhile, so get used to the place."

That statement about being bait deflected some of Cory's immediate fears for his life, and he ventured to ask a question. "How do you speak better English than anyone else I've met here?"

The withered old Garlian stared off, unfocused for a minute, then he turned and started to walk away.

Calling back over his shoulder, he replied, "I spent ten years on your world. They were not pleasant years, believe me. I was not treated well at all."

Mike and Doug stepped through the doorway and it immediately closed behind them. "I'm not so sure I like that," Doug said.

Mike nodded. "Me either. Let's be careful now."

They found themselves in another corridor with the eerie diffused light.

"Go forward or turn back?" Doug asked.

"We know what's in store for us if we turn back. And that's assuming we can open the door from this side. So let's go on."

Doug gave the thumbs up and gestured for Mike to take the lead.

The tunnel was short. Once they walked around a bend, it ended abruptly at another dead end.

"Think like Brad?" Mike questioned.

Doug grinned. "Why stop when it's worked so far?"

Mike stepped right up to the wall barring their progress and searched with his eyes while running his hands over where he suspected there'd be some sort of hidden switch.

"I feel the slight outline of a door but can't find the release mechanism like the door we just passed through."

Doug watched Mike for a few more minutes then said, "Let me try. Fresh set of eyes might help."

Doug began running his hands along the hidden door's outline. After a few minutes, he shook his head, frowning. "I don't feel anything either."

Mike slapped him on the back and laughed. "Brad did it again."

Doug turned around. "What?"

Mike pointed to the right side wall and stepped over to it. "I decided that Brad would give up quickly when he couldn't find a release on the outline of the door itself. He'd look elsewhere. Bingo." Mike pressed a small square area, barely distinguishable from the surrounding wall.

The door in front of Doug slid silently open.

"We're getting pretty good at this," Doug said, grinning.

Mike was looking up. "How many stories would you say this underground city has?" he asked, stunned by what he was seeing.

Doug too was staring upwards, speechless until he said finally, "Don't know. Maybe a dozen— maybe less, maybe more."

"But we agree that from where we are, or were, we should have had to walk up steps to get out into the open, right?"

"Brad made it clear that he was going to take everyone to a set of stairs to escape the Ancients. Yeah."

"Then how is it possible that we just stepped through that door and we're out into fresh air? We should have been as many as a dozen stories below ground level." Mike said, looking at Doug.

"Beats me."

The two of them were standing just beyond the doorway they'd opened. Spread out in front of them was clear blue sky and a riotous profusion of jungle-like growth. A cacophony of chirping insect sounds and bird calls, and a smell that reminded Mike of the tropics, assaulted their senses. While they were standing there staring, three brightly colored parrot-like birds rose out of the growth and fluttered off in a stunning display of color.

Mike turned around to stare at the doorway gaping open behind them. "Only one answer. The doorway has to be a portal. There's nothing behind us but more jungle, except the door."

"That's it, has to be. I can see the tunnel inside the door but it disappears around the bend."

Mike scratched his chin. "What do we do? I wasn't expecting this when we decided to keep going through the door."

"Well, it's clear we can't go forward and get back to everyone. We have no idea where this is. It doesn't even look like we're still on the Empty World, does it?"

Mike nodded. "It looks and smells more like Earth, if you ask me."

"Well let's look around a bit then. We can head back after that and face the issue of the Ancients looking for us in the city."

"Sounds like a plan. This is too intriguing to just turn around right away," Mike said, gesturing ahead of them. "Let's mark the route we take or we'll get lost for sure."

Doug nodded. He pulled out a knife and knelt down to scratch a three foot diameter circle in the ground, right in front of the door. "Might just as well start right here. I'll mark some trees as we go too. In case it rains."

Mike pointed to the left of where they were standing. "That could be a trail. See the gap in the foliage?"

Entering through that gap in the foliage, they found themselves in deep shadows, the trees forming an almost impenetrable canopy over their heads. The trail they began to follow was well worn, with little or no new growth to hamper their progress. Animal screams periodically pierced the air, intruding on the nearly constant buzzing and rustling noises that emanated from either side of the trail. The air was stagnant, and smelled heavily of decaying vegetation.

After half an hour of walking, Mike stopped. Doug took a couple steps then turned and came back.

"I don't think this is Earth, despite the similarities," Mike said.

"What makes you think that?"

"The smell. Even though it's definitely tropical smelling, there's a scent I can't place that is very unusual. We're not on the Empty World either though, based on that blue sky we saw before hitting this trail. And that bothers me too. Who made this trail?"

"Yeah, I'm wondering that too," Doug agreed, then closed his eyes and took a deep breath in through his nose.

"Cheese. It reminds me of cheddar cheese." He smiled. "Of course it's mixed with the smell of rotting leaves."

Mike sniffed the air. "You're right, now that you identify it. It does smell a bit like cheese."

They started walking again and continued for another half an hour without a break in the canopy or any sign of side trails.

"Well, what do you think?" Mike asked.

"Let's keep going for a bit then turn around after an hour, no matter what we find. This won't get us back to the kids or help us find Cory. We're stuck heading back the way we came and trying to dodge the Ancients."

Mike nodded.

They pushed on, a sheen of sweat building up on their skin from the heavy tropical heat. Just as they were about to give up and turn around, the trail widened considerably, so curiosity forced them to press onward, even though the agreed upon hour had passed. Breaks in the overhead foliage let in spears of sunlight that turned the trail into a patchwork of light and dark. Finally the trail they walked was bathed in complete sunshine, the jungle receding from overhead and revealing blue sky.

Doug pointed ahead and stopped. "It looks like the trail ends and the jungle closes in."

"Yes, but there's something else there, not just more jungle. Let's see what it is."

They walked the hundred yards or so to the end of the trail and stopped. The jungle was a massive wall in front of them. Vines and tall grasses twisted around spindly trees, and everywhere there were colorful blooms and bright green foliage. But there was something other than jungle, almost obscured by the unchecked growth and the passage of time.

Mike was speechless at the sight of what towered over them. Doug shook his head, prompted to speak in a whisper by the sheer grandeur of what they were looking at.

"I've seen pictures, but I've never seen anything this magnificent. Have you?"

CHAPTER 11

"**I** thought we were going to stay away from this forest," Danny signed as they took a break. The forest loomed up ahead, casting deep, menacing shadows.

Christy looked over at Brad, who was shifting from one foot to the other and staring into the forest.

"I guess we have no choice. Brad wouldn't be leading us this way if it wasn't the only way to go," Christy said and signed.

Brad turned away from the forest. "Around, not into. We shouldn't go in," he said.

Danny, who'd read Brad's lips, exhaled the breath he'd been holding. "Well, that's a relief," he said. "That's one scary looking forest."

Jack stood apart from the others and took a few steps closer to the dark mass ahead. Even without wind or debilitating sound, the forest was still a sinister looking tangle of ancient growth. "Scary is right, Danny," Jack said. "I'm glad we're going around."

They rested in silence until Brad roused himself from staring off into the gloom; he turned to his left and bolted off without a word.

"There he goes again," Jack said, shaking his head as he began to follow. Christy and Danny hurried behind.

Suddenly, after Brad led them at a quick pace for a while, he stopped just as suddenly as he'd started.

"Mistake, mistake, mistake," Brad mumbled, then crouched down and wrapped his arms around his knees, burying his face.

Christy crouched down next to Brad and tentatively touched him on the shoulder.

"What's a mistake, Brad?"

Brad lifted his head and bounced up, walking briskly forward for a dozen steps then stopping.

"I think I know what he means," Jack said, pointing.

They'd been following a clear path that skirted the edge of the forest. At first it seemed her grandfather was pointing at more of the same short grass, but as Christy kept watching, it turned into something else.

Another trail, perpendicular to the one they were following, was blocking their path. As they stared at it, it started to flow: a moving belt of grasses, dirt, and rubble, feeding right into the forest they were trying to avoid.

"It looks like a moving river of dirt," Danny said and signed.

"Looks a lot like a river of quicksand to me. But a minute ago it was barely moving. Now it's picked up speed," Jack said.

"How's that possible?" Danny asked.

Jack shrugged. "Danny, you've been here long enough to see many strange things, just add this river of dirt to that list."

"Brad?" Christy asked. "Is there a way around this?"

Brad shook his head. "Wait."

Brad was the closest to the phenomenon. He spread his arms out at his sides and gestured the others behind him to move back, without taking his eyes off the flowing dirt river.

They all stepped back several steps, waiting for whatever else Brad might say or do. The river was slowing, it seemed. Suddenly, it was completely still again, resembling the harmless trail it had originally looked like from a distance.

Without warning them, Brad suddenly bolted across the now-stationary dirt and disappeared down the continuation of the trail he'd been leading them on.

"Let's go!" Jack shouted, waving Christy and Danny forward.

The two of them raced ahead. Jack stopped right in the middle of the now solid ground and waved them past him.

"Hurry, we don't know how long we've got before this starts flowing again," Jack urged.

Once Christy and Danny had reached stable ground, he started after them.

Christy turned to wait for him. Just as he was almost level with them, the dirt began to flow again, but faster than before, like a river moving over rapids. Jack sunk in up to his knees, shouting out a curse as the flowing ground gripped him into its current.

Christy screamed and started to run back to him.

"No, Christy! Stay there. It's too dangerous. Go after Brad— don't lose him!" They watched as Jack struggled to free himself unsuccessfully. The more he struggled, the deeper he sank into the flowing mass of dirt. Christy screamed again as her grandfather was pulled farther away from her. Within seconds, he was gone from sight, whisked off into the bowels of the forest.

Christy cried right where she was. Danny wept with her, feeling the loss deeply too. But Danny also had to keep Brad from going on ahead. Several times, Christy watched with indifference born of her grief as Danny took off at a run after Brad and gently talked him back.

After nearly half an hour of nonstop crying, Danny came over to her and hugged her. That brought a new intensity to both of their grieving until Brad slipped off again.

Danny backed out of the hug. Thinking he needed to get Christy up and moving, he said, "We'd better go after him."

Christy lifted her head, watching Brad's receding figure, not caring. "I can't go on anymore, I've had it." She whispered her voice thick from the crying.

Danny shook his head, not following her lips. But when she didn't move to get up, he wiped his eyes and ran to catch up to Brad and bring him back again.

Cory was alone. He was locked in a rickety, old, wooden building with a rusted gate secured across the entrance. Cory knew that it was not a good sign that the old Garlian, who referred to himself as Randle, had not enjoyed the ten years he'd apparently spent on Earth.

"That's not good, Murray, not at all. If that withered old raisin wasn't treated good on Earth, I don't like my chan —sorry— *our* chances here." Cory was patting Murray nervously and paused for a moment in thought. "It's 'well,' not 'good.' The old raisin wasn't treated *well*." He sighed. "That's for you mom, since you're not here to correct my grammar."

Scratching Murray behind the ears, he continued speaking. "It looks like you're not the ace in the hole I was hoping you'd be, my friend."

All of a sudden, small chips of the wooden ceiling came splintering down onto Murray. Cory frowned and looked up.

Peeking through a two foot diameter hole in the ceiling was a small, bald head, smaller than a Garlian's even— only about the size of a softball. A pair of enormous purple eyes stared back at Cory. They took up about a quarter of the whole face and were accompanied by tiny ears, no nose, and a mouth that seemed to just melt, lipless, into the greenish skin.

Suddenly a squeaky voice came out of that mouth.

"What are you? I heard you speaking this language, so it must be yours, but I've never seen the likes of you before. I know of 'The Old Ones' and 'The Hard Shells,' and of course 'The Meanies.'"

For several minutes, all Cory could do was stare. The head was odd enough as it was, sticking upside down out of the ceiling with its awkward disproportionate features, but to hear it speaking English? That took Cory completely by surprise.

"Come on, I know you can speak. I heard you," the creature said. "Unless that furry thing on your lap who you call Murray is the brains of the outfit."

Cory wheeled backwards a few feet so he wouldn't have to look up at such a sharp angle.

"How can you know English if you don't know what I am?"

The creature didn't reply at first. Instead his two arms came through the hole and he used them to pull himself through the hole, doing a neat flip to land on his feet on the floor. It startled Murray who stood up and hissed.

"Settle down, Murray," Cory said, gripping the cat tighter and stroking his back to calm him.

The creature was only three feet tall and slender. He wore an orange, one-piece suit that left only his head and his small, three-fingered hands bare. Maybe it was the size of the creature, but the outfit reminded Cory of a pair of footie pajamas.

The creature took a step closer. "I'm not speaking English. You're hearing English. I'm telepathic. I'm speaking directly into your speech centers and you hear me in your own language. Neat, huh?"

Cory nodded, wary of the light and breezy attitude of the creature. "Why are you here? Just to find out what I am?"

"That mostly. I'm curious. So what are you?"

"My name is Cory. I'm human. What's your name and what are you?"

The creature stared down at the floor. "I and my brother are the last of our species. We are known as uTaube. But once he and I are gone, that's it ... Poof! We'll all be gone." The creature put his tiny hands up to his face, covered his eyes and started to sob. It quickly escalated into wracking wails, his little body heaving with wave after wave of tears.

Cory wheeled himself backwards a few feet; he was unsure of what to make of the creature balling his eyes out in front of him.

Abruptly the crying stopped and the creature dropped his hands. He stared at Cory with those deep purple eyes. "That get to you?"

"Huh?"

"Pretty good, wasn't it?" The creature's lipless mouth creeped up at the corners into a smile.

"You were joking about your own species' extinction?"

"No, it's true. We're the last that I know of. That doesn't mean I can't go for the dramatic scene."

"You are strange." Cory shook his head. "You haven't told me your name yet."

"I'm Poov the Great. Poov the Beast Trainer, they used to call me."

Cory didn't know what he was expecting, but that wasn't it. He started laughing so hard that Murray jumped off his lap and began circling around the wheelchair.

"Poov the Great? Poov the Beast Trainer? You have got to be kidding me." When Cory finally calmed down and stopped laughing, Murray leaped back up into his lap and settled down as if he'd never left.

"It's not humorous. I earned my names. I'm a legend amongst my people," Poov said, pausing to take a deep breath. "Except they're all gone." He stood silent, his face sad.

"What's your brother's name?"

"He's Utoov the Keeper, Utoov the Protector. He is much more important than I am."

"Why?"

The little creature paced back and forth. "He guards a very important place. It holds all knowledge of this world's history and representative versions of all its past technology. You would call the building a pyramid. It also harbors a twin portal to every portal ever created on this world. Utoov is so important because he has to keep all that power out of the hands of Ancients today. They can't get a hold of it."

Cory was only mildly curious about why Utoov needed to keep the pyramid out of the hands of the Ancients. But he was very interested in … "Portals? You say there are portals there?"

Poov nodded.

"How do you get to this pyramid?"

"It's on another world."

"Oh." Cory was crushed, his momentary hopes dashed.

"There's a portal in Abuuenki to it."

"Outstanding." Cory clapped his hands together, startling Murray for a second.

Poov seemed to lose interest in Cory all of a sudden, because he rushed over to the back wall. Pressing something hidden, one of the patched spots on the wall creaked open.

"I'm sorry, I have to go," Poov said, disappearing through the wall and pulling the patch shut behind him.

Cory wheeled over to the wall, searching for whatever Poov had pressed to open the hole. Finally he found the small indentation. HIs fingers were way too big to fit in so he reached under his seat and rummaged through the pack he had. Using a pen tip he pressed the spot. The wooden patch creaked open again. Cory examined it for a minute then closed it, throwing up his hands in disgust.

"Well, Murray, that would be our way out if I could walk or crawl. Even if I don't know where this leads I'd take it in a heartbeat."

Cory thought for second, snapped his fingers and wheeled himself in a small circle. "Wait a minute ... I do know where this leads! I bet this escape hole is the same one that the Garlians use to break their friends out. It must lead to under the town. This has to be the same cell that they stick everyone they capture into. We'd be as good as rescued except for the fact that I can't follow if Ufei sends a rescue party."

Cory lowered his head. "Murray, I don't understand. I guess Ufei and the rest don't know about the hidden mechanism that pops open this patch to the tunnel or they wouldn't have had to wait for someone to rescue them."

He cupped his hands and shouted at the patch covering the hole Poov had disappeared through. "Thank you, Poov." Then he lowered his voice, talking to Murray again. "If I ever get out of here, I have some valuable info for the Garlians."

"Magnificent barely describes it," Mike said.

"What do you think? Egyptian or Mayan?" Doug asked.

"Looks a bit more like a Mayan pyramid than an Egyptian one to me. But even that doesn't seem accurate. At least not based on what I've seen in pictures and a documentary or two over the years."

Doug nodded, not taking his eyes off the thing. "It looks as if the jungle has tried to claim it, but despite that, it's still in excellent condition. I don't think I remember seeing any pyramids with these vivid colors still visible on them, do you?"

"No, I agree. These colors aren't like what I've seen on artistic recreations of the Mayan pyramids. Those are predominately blue and red if I recall. This is gold and silver and purple. If Christy were here, we'd get some stunning pictures, I'm sure."

Doug nodded. "This hardly shows any decay at all. And the weather is as tropical as any I know of! Plus the growth crawling all over it should have taken a toll as well, but it hasn't. How tall do you think it is?"

"Seventy, eighty feet maybe," Mike guessed.

"Looks bigger than that to me. I bet it's one hundred feet. Easily." Mike turned to Doug. "What do you say we explore more closely?"

"You couldn't keep me away. After you, my friend."

CHAPTER 12

Christy's mood alternated between grief and anger: grief over her grandfather being swept away from them, and anger over how it happened. If her grandfather had just crossed the unstable ground with them instead of waiting for her and Danny to get across, he'd still be with them.

"Christy?" Danny touched her arm gently. When she didn't respond, he spoke his mind regardless. "You can't give up. We can't give up. We have to keep going on."

Christy lifted her head and turned so Danny could read her lips. "I know. I'm sorry, I didn't mean it. I just need a few more minutes, please."

Danny nodded, squeezing her arm in support.

Brad, who was standing off by himself but had finally stopped running ahead, walked over to Christy and sat down next to her. "He kept you safe. That's all he wanted. He's gone now."

Christy put her hand to her mouth, stifling a cry. Danny noticed the movement. "What?" he signed.

She signed back: "Brad just said that my grandfather just wanted to keep us safe."

Danny nodded. "Wow. Interesting. Brad doesn't speak up often."

Christy agreed but couldn't bring herself to tell him what else Brad had said that had prompted her reaction.

Brad's attempt to communicate shook Christy out of her lethargy and pushed her grief aside enough that she finally agreed to keep going.

They walked for hours, Brad in the lead slightly and Christy and Danny walking side by side. Eventually breaking out of a narrow, shady section of the trail into a sun-filled stretch, the path widened considerably. Christy wiped sweat off her brow then stopped walking, sitting down on a large boulder and closing her eyes.

Danny stopped next to her. "Brad, wait, come back here," he called out. "Let's stop and rest. Christy's had enough for today."

"Thanks, Danny," she signed, looking at him then closing her eyes again.

Christy kept her head down. A few seconds later, seemingly right in her ear, she heard Brad say, "Not here, come on."

Christy tried to ignore him until he gently took her hand and pulled her up. "Not here."

Christy couldn't believe it; Brad had initiated human touch. She'd never seen that before. Brad had occasionally surprised her with eye contact, but not touch, until now.

Danny was staring wide-eyed. "What did he say?"

She turned so Danny could read her lips. "He said not to rest here."

Brad continued to guide her by the hand. Christy and Danny just shrugged at each other and followed.

For the next hour, Brad never let go of Christy's hand. He set a fast pace that Danny struggled to keep up with. Christy just had to go with the flow, letting Brad guide them to whatever end he had in mind.

Finally, when the trail narrowed again and the shadows became deep and the air cool, Brad stopped and let her hand go. "Here we can rest."

Danny joined them, panting from the exertion of keeping up. "What now?" he signed and spoke.

"Good question. Brad, do you know where this leads?" Christy asked.

Brad held his hand out. Christy frowned at him until Danny said, "The camera. I think he's asking for the camera again."

Christy swung her pack off her back and rummaged in a side pocket. "Is this what you want?"

Brad took it without comment and turned it on, then turned to the back screen and began scrolling through pictures.

"Looks like that was it." Danny grinned.

Brad thrust the back screen of the camera so close to Christy's face that she had to lean away from it. She took the camera from him and stared at the screen. It was a portion of the photo she'd taken of the map mural. Brad had zoomed in on a section. "What am I looking at, Brad?"

"Cory will be there."

"But, Brad, how do you know that?"

"Cory will be there." Brad turned away from her and hung his head, mumbling to himself.

"Please Brad. What do you mean?" Christy asked.

Danny tapped Christy on the shoulder and held up his hand for her to stop. He got Brad's attention and started signing with him. Brad responded until a question from Danny caused him to shake his head no, and he turned away, mumbling again.

Danny gestured Christy over to him and held his finger to his lips so Brad would not overhear. Before he could speak, Christy asked, "Did Brad answer you with complete sentences? I couldn't follow much because you both were signing too fast but it seemed like that's what happened. He does so much better at signing than expressing himself speaking, doesn't he?"

Danny nodded. "He knows that Cory didn't take the portal that Tarynn tricked us into using. He thinks she sent him outside the city, somehow convincing him that she knew where he could find more devices. There's only one small settlement near that city on the map, which is what he showed us in the photo." Danny glanced again at Brad, who was still not paying them any mind. "I still don't know how Brad came to the conclusion about where Cory is. That doesn't add up to me. Just because Brad thinks Tarynn was telling us lies doesn't mean Cory's where he thinks."

Christy stared at Danny until he held his gaze unwaveringly on her. "We have no other plan, Danny. Brad's in charge of where we're going. Have you ever seen him be wrong so far?"

Danny shook his head but signed just out of Brad's sight. "No, you're right, but there's always a first time."

It had been an hour since Poov disappeared from his cell. Cory wheeled up to the metal gate of his prison room and pressed his face against the bars, straining to see down the corridor.

"Hey, Randle ...you there?" Cory shouted.

He waited for a response but none came.

Shrugging, he wheeled away from the gate toward the back wall. Just as he was about to open the hidden patch door that Poov had disappeared through, Randle arrived at the gate.

"What? Why did you call me?"

"How long are you going to keep me here?"

"As long as it takes to lure a rescue party."

Cory, emboldened by the fact that he was seemingly not in danger of being killed, decided to search for more information.

"What makes you think someone will come to rescue me?"

"They always do." Randle turned to leave but Cory held up his hands.

"Wait," he said. "We call you people Garlians because that's what the computer in one of the cities called you. What do you call yourselves?"

"Just as you are known as Humans, we are known as Gyrlees."

Cory repeated the name, stumbling over the pronunciation, and Randle smiled at the attempt before resuming his angry snarl.

"How come the Gyrlees in the cities I've seen are like little kids, running around in packs and tearing up everything they find? They don't seem smart like you."

Randle was silent and his face became even angrier. Cory thought he wasn't going to get an answer but the old Garlian took a deep breath and spoke.

"They are the lost ones," he said. "There is no hope for them. Someday I hope to answer your question for myself."

Randle fell silent again and turned, walking down the corridor and out of sight.

"Whoa, Murray. We hit a sore spot. So, there's something creepy going on with the Garlians in the cities."

Cory sat still and stroked Murray's back as the cat purred his approval.

"I wonder how Randle's going to know when someone comes for me. Assuming someone does, that is. They probably don't have cameras but maybe someone is watching me."

Cory spun his wheelchair in a circle. "Hey, who's watching?" he called out. He waited, but nobody answered or came. Cory kept spinning slowly, thinking as he did. "Hey Randle! You must have seen Poov come and go, so you must know that eventually the Garlians under the town are going to figure out how to get back into the tunnels from this room."

When he didn't hear or see anyone coming, he gave up thinking Randle would return. "Pssst! Up here," a voice called.

He looked up and Poov's head was peaking down through the ceiling again. The funny looking creature was grinning, but upside down it looked like a thin, lipless frown.

"Why did you leave and why are you back?"

Instead of answering, Poov looked startled. "You've got company coming," he said.

The next second, the tiny head disappeared and Cory heard footsteps. When he turned, Randle was approaching.

The old Garlian unlocked the metal gate and entered, walking straight across to the hidden entrance and pushed his slim finger into the spot that opened it. The door popped open.

"As you can see," Randle began, "I know about this." He closed the door, then called out loudly in his own language.

He turned, staring triumphantly at Cory. "Now watch," he said.

Putting his slim finger again into the indentation he grinned as nothing happened. The door remained closed.

"This opens when I allow it to, and only when I allow it to." His grin was vicious as he stared at Cory, judging his reaction.

Cory stared back at him then turned his head away.

"Look at me," Randle commanded.

When Cory complied, the old Garlian said, "There is someone coming here to see you. When I told him I had a human here, he wanted to take a look at you."

Footsteps echoed from down the corridor and around the bend. "Ah," said Randle, "here he comes now."

Cory wheeled around to look and stifled a cry of fear as he saw TuMaz Tan, Angry Ancient as Christy called him, round the corner and head toward his cell. Here was the Ancient who had killed Clacker and started the war on Clacker's species, the Cleaners. He would certainly remember Cory, and that wouldn't be good.

"Hopefully whoever created this path and the pyramid will be friendly," Mike said as he snapped off several vines that blocked their path.

"We can hope, but let's assume anyone we meet won't be friendly," Doug suggested. "Better still, let's not meet anyone if we can help it."

Doug slashed at the tall reeds that had taken root around the entire perimeter of the pyramid with his knife. After nearly an hour of sweaty, exhausting clearing, they were rewarded for their hard work and stood finally at the base of the pyramid, which towered over them.

"We were wrong, I think," Doug said.

Mike was shaking his head in disbelief. "You got that right. All the gold and silver that we thought was paint looks like it actually is gold and silver metal. But what's the purple? It sparkles when the light hits it. Or them, rather; there must be thousands of small stones on the surface of this thing."

"Could be a mineral. Maybe something like amethyst."

Mike shrugged. He noticed a small purple gem in the dirt at his feet and bent down to pick it up.

"Well, this must have come off the surface. Maybe we'll get a chance to take this to someone back home and have them tell us what it is."

"Home. I hope we all get back there," Doug said wistfully.

"We will. The kids are amazingly resourceful, as we've seen too many times to count. And don't forget, we left them with Jack."

Doug was quiet for a moment, then said, "Let's see what's here and then get back so we can find them."

Mike nodded. "We need to find an entrance to this. Must be on one of the three sides we haven't seen yet."

They started following along the edge of the pyramid, and as soon as they hit the first corner and turned toward the second side, Doug stopped them.

"This angle isn't ninety degrees. That leads me to think that this isn't a square base, maybe five sides not four."

"A five sided pyramid? Have you ever heard of that?" Mike asked.

"I haven't, but then I've never been a real history or architecture buff, so who knows?"

"Look!" Mike said, pointing at a darkly shadowed entrance dead center along the wall. There were considerably less vines and other growth clinging to the entrance side. An obvious path led off into the jungle directly opposite of it.

"Too bad we didn't stumble into this side first," Mike said, chuckling.

"Oh, well, live and learn."

Suddenly Mike held up his arm. "Shhhh, hear that?" he whispered.

"Hear what?" Doug hissed.

But immediately, he heard it himself. Coming from the entrance was the faint sound of voices chanting. Many deep voices.

CHAPTER 13

"**W**ell, we know where he's headed, even if we don't catch up to him," Christy said.

"True, but do we know we're on the right path?" Danny had given up signing and was speaking as they hurried along the trail that Brad had disappeared down.

"As long as we don't come across any forks in this path, we should be ok," Christy replied.

"We can't be sure of that."

Desperate to catch up with Brad, they continued at a jog. Suddenly, Danny stopped completely and dropped to the ground, utterly exhausted. He rested his head on his hands and started to cry.

Christy slowly slid down beside him, just as tired. She ignored his crying for a few minutes but when it didn't stop, she wrapped an arm around him.

"I'm sorry, Christy," Danny said. He leaned into Christy's hug.

She squeezed a bit harder and then let go. "I know it's not fair that you were forced to come back," Christy signed. "I'm sorry about that. But I'm glad you're here."

Danny wiped his eyes and managed a smile. "Thanks. Funny, you told me that Trevor said it wasn't fair he had to go home. And it's not fair I was forced to come back. I'd gladly switch places with him and he'd gladly switch with me, I'd bet."

Christy nodded. "You're right, he would."

After that, neither of them said anything, even as they continued on the path. Another hour went by and they still hadn't caught sight of Brad. Soon the scenery began changing and they started to see signs of ruins. Concrete, or something similar, was dotting the ground in broken, black-lichen covered pieces. Clearings appeared in greater frequency. Moss covered mounds in odd geometric shapes filled each clearing they passed and hinted at a civilization even further in the past than the broken concrete.

Soon the path widened and became a jumbled mess of broken pavement. Christy knelt down and examined a small piece that had become dislodged. "It's rubbery," she said. "And it has sparkly things imbedded in it." She handed it to Danny who looked at it and nodded, then tossed it aside.

Christy was just about to comment on a growing hum when Danny said, "I feel a vibration under us."

"I think it's coming from somewhere up ahead," Christy said, pointing in the direction of the humming sound. They continued on, heading toward it.

Trevor walked slowly to Ginny Wentworth's house. He hoped talking to her would help his mood. Since he'd been back, he hadn't been able to get over his anger about Christy betraying him for a second time. She'd backed the adults' decision to make him come home, and that hurt.

On top of the anger, he also felt totally isolated. His mom had had to withdraw him from school while he was in the Empty World, and had set up tutors for him since his return. She planned to homeschool him for the rest of the year and let him return to school the following fall. He never thought he'd miss going to school, but he did, very much so.

As he knocked on Ginny's front door, he wondered how everyone else's parents had explained their absences.

"Come in Trevor," Mrs. Wentworth said, opening the door and stepping aside. "Go on up, you know the way," she added, smiling.

"Thanks, Mrs. Wentworth."

He climbed the stairs to Ginny's room and walked in.

"Hey," he said, sitting down on the edge of her bed. She got up from her desk and gave him a hug. He let her this time. "Hey. How you doing?" she asked.

"I've been better. It's good to see you."

"Same here." She paused a second then said, "I'm sorry you had to come back."

He snorted. "Thanks."

"At least you got to go. I'd give anything to have been there. Tell me everything."

Trevor spent the next hour and a half telling Ginny about his experiences, only leaving out his own heroics in saving Christy's dad. Ginny shook her head, amazed at the stories he told. "But you left out how you rescued Mr. Walker," she said, squeezing his hand. "Detective Lockhart told my mom about it before he went back."

Trevor smiled but shrugged off the implied praise. "I didn't know you guys got the chance to talk to the detective."

"Come on, of course we heard about it when you got back and went to see Cory's mom. My mom and I wanted to know what was going on."

Trevor frowned and pulled his hand out of Ginny's. "Well, now all I can do is wait. I'm useless here."

Ginny looked at him and her lips were pursed. Trevor could tell she was annoyed. "Well, as I said, you at least have been there. I haven't had the chance. I'd go in a heartbeat." Trevor grinned at her.

"I'm sorry, you're right. I shouldn't complain. It's just that, I was there and never should have let everyone talk me into coming back. I mean, what could they have done if I'd refused?"

Ginny smiled. "Well we're both here now being useless. So ... tell me what you're planning. You must be planning something."

Trevor shook his head. "I wish I was, but it's too late to use the pond. There aren't going to be any more thunderstorms till next June at least. And the detective took the devices back with him, so we're kind of stuck here."

"There goes our plan of checking out the pyramid. I don't want to run into whoever is chanting," Mike whispered.

"Agreed. Let's get back to the portal," Doug replied.

They quickly traced their steps back along the trail until the pyramid was far behind them. When they were a safe distance away from the pyramid, they stopped to rest for a while.

"We should discuss what we're going to do when we step through the portal back to the city," Doug said. "We'll probably be chased as soon as we leave the alleyway."

"Run as fast as we can," Mike said, grinning.

"Well, yeah, that's a given, but we only know the general direction we should head to. Hopefully we'll see the stairs before we see the Ancients."

As they started walking again, Mike said, "I was thinking ... when you and I decided to come after the kids, we should have taken weapons with us. Stupid of me not to at least suggest it. It would have made this so much easier. We wouldn't have to be discussing worrying about Ancients chasing us right now."

Doug dismissed the thought with a wave. "Well, it's too late now. But there've definitely been a few times I've wished we had them too."

They continued following the marks Doug had cut into the saplings until they finally came to the clearing where Doug had hastily scratched a circle on the ground in front of the portal doorway. The circle was there, but the portal wasn't.

TuMaz came within sight of Cory and his eyes widened. A vicious grin spread across his horselike face. He stood in front of the metal bars and spoke a stream of unintelligible words.

Randle nodded, bowing slightly. When TuMaz turned and walked away, the sneer on the old Garlian's lips and the hatred in his eyes told Cory that there was no love lost between the old Garlian and the Ancient.

"He wondered if you had seriously hurt yourself when he escaped your companions during the confusion. Now he sees that you have and his comment was 'It serves you right.'" Randle sneered at Cory and paused a moment in thought. "I've changed my mind about you," the Garlian said with a vicious grin.

Cory took the bait. "What do you mean?"

"I'm going to have you killed."

Randle sneered again and called out in his language before stepping out of Cory's prison. After making a show of loudly closing and locking the metal bars, he strode off down the corridor.

Cory started to cry, his fear now all-consuming. Murray stood up in his lap and licked his face. Cory responded with a weak smile before ignoring the cat completely and resuming his crying.

"Pssst!"

Cory looked up to see Poov's head peeking through the ceiling.

"You're in a right bad pickle if you ask me," the creature said, actually sounding concerned despite the cavalier way he described Cory's death sentence.

Cory wiped his eyes but didn't say anything. Poov slid down, doing his acrobatic flip and landing just in front of Cory. He had changed into a dark gray jumpsuit, a decided improvement over the gaudy orange one.

"Can you push yourself?"

Cory frowned, not understanding why Poov was asking. "Of course."

The creature nodded and walked over to the metal bars, fiddling with something. Within seconds, the door swung open.

"Well, don't just sit there," Poov said, his face set in a grim smile. "Let's go! They're going to kill you."

As Cory followed Poov out, he asked, "How are we going to get past the guard? They probably have someone around the bend in the corridor."

"We're not. That pompous fool, Randle, doesn't know everything about this place, but I do."

Stopping a few feet along the corridor, Poov bent down to the line between the floor and the wall and within seconds, a door slid silently back, revealing a tunnel on the other side.

"Go!" Poov commanded. "I have to stay on this side. The secret door can't be closed from inside the tunnel."

Cory hesitated, a million questions running through his mind.

"Hurry, they will have seen us leave the cell, but they don't have eyes on the corridor here so they won't know how you avoided them. The tunnel will get you back to your friends under the city."

Cory wheeled into the tunnel and Poov did something that slid the door silently back to its closed position. Cory was all alone, but the tunnel was dimly lit so he could see enough to get around. He spun around, ready to leave, when he heard muffled cries on the other side. It sounded like the guards had seen Poov. Hoping Poov was right about them not knowing about this secret to the tunnels, he tried to make out what was happening on the other side.

He heard Poov's distinctive voice yelling in what must have been Garlian. Then he heard several shouts from someone who was not Poov. The next thing he heard was a horrible shriek and a gurgling sound, and then silence.

Afraid to move for fear of his wheelchair somehow making a noise loud enough to be heard on the other side of the hidden door, he waited. Muffled voices could be heard briefly, then a dragging sound mixed with a couple of voices laughing, which quickly grew faint until all was silent.

"Should we hop on?" Christy signed to Danny.

They'd come to a moving road; it was in terrible condition but seemed to still be working. It reminded Christy of a large conveyor belt. Christy looked at her camera and the map.

"This has to be where Brad thinks Cory went, based on what I'm looking at on the map," Christy said. Her hands were occupied scrolling around the Empty World map and enlarging and minimizing sections of it, but Danny had no problem reading her lips.

He replied by saying aloud, "We really haven't seen any other path that Brad could have taken, and this should still be heading to wherever Brad ran off to."

Christy stepped onto the moving path and reached a hand to Danny.

"All aboard," he said, laughing as she pulled him up.

They traveled for a long time. In some spots, the beltway wasn't working and they had to walk across to the next moving section. Ahead of them a town was visible at the end of the road. It was nothing like the underground cities they'd seen. This was a dilapidated mishmash of wooden structures, cobbled together haphazardly. Occasionally they could glimpse a more sophisticated structure poking out through the tangle of wooden construction.

"If you told me that was built by a team of madmen, I'd believe it," Christy said. The settlement loomed larger with each second.

They came to another section of the beltway that wasn't working and began to walk across it.

"Christy! Danny!" a voice called out to them. It wasn't Brad's voice. It was female and very high-pitched.

Christy grabbed Danny's arm to get his attention and signed as fast as she could. "Someone just called our names. It wasn't Brad." She pointed off into the jumble of growth to the side of the beltway.

"How's that possible?" Danny signed.

Christy shrugged as she stepped off the beltway, motioning Danny to follow her. She headed toward where she'd heard their names.

"To your left," the same voice called to them.

Christy prodded Danny and pointed to their left, though she didn't see anyone.

Danny squinted and then excitedly ran forward, beckoning Christy along behind him. He darted around some moss-covered debris and stopped short, scratching his head. He threw up his hands and spun all the way around in a three-hundred-sixty degree turn.

"I saw something or someone here, I'm sure of it," he said, shaking his head.

Christy shrugged, scanning the area for whoever'd called their names. Just when they both were ready to give up, a Garlian girl stepped out from behind a tree and pointed farther off to where it looked like the ground was lifting up. A lid was opening up to an entrance underground. The girl ran to it, glancing behind to make sure Christy and Danny were following.

They followed the girl through the entrance and onto what turned out to be a ramp that dipped underground. When the ramp leveled into a tunnel, the girl stopped and rushed back to close the lid. They were now in complete darkness.

The girl's footsteps got louder as she came back down the ramp. Christy was overwhelmed by the sudden events.

"How do you know our names?" she asked when the footsteps had stopped.

"Brad told me you'd be coming along."

CHAPTER 14

"Ok, how can this be?" Doug said, scratching his head. "How can the portal just be gone?"

"It can't be. There has to be some other explanation," Mike replied.

"But we followed the marks I made. We couldn't have gotten lost." Doug stopped short, his breath catching in his throat.

"What?" Mike asked, noticing Doug's hesitation.

Instead of answering, Doug retraced their steps to the edge of the clearing and knelt down, reaching for a sapling. He inspected the cut he'd made, bending the supple tree in his fingers. He paused for a moment and stared off down the path. "Mike," he said finally, "look at this cut. I'm not sure, but the angle of it doesn't seem consistent with what I think I made when we first came through."

He let the sapling spring back and stood next to it, withdrawing his knife and bending his knees as he fit it into the cut.

Doug shook his head. "It not only is angled wrong based on how I would have cut it, but it's lower on the tree. I would have had to bend down to make this cut and I didn't do that when I made all the marks to guide us back. I've been a bit uneasy for the last hour or so because I thought something was slightly wrong with the marks we've been following, but it seemed so impossible that I just ignored it."

"Are you sure?" Mike asked.

"Yes. Well … I think so. But if these aren't my marks, what have we been following?"

"And if we haven't been following the marks *you* cut, then who made these and pointed them to this clearing, and copied the circle you drew? And why?" Mike asked.

"And how do we get back to the portal?" Doug added. "We're going to have to search for my marks. If we can't find them, we're lost," he said.

Just then, a cackling laugh echoed through the trees, rising in intensity. Mike groaned and covered his ears. Doug fell onto his knees and did the same.

Within seconds, the laughter stopped. Doug tentatively removed his hands and stood up. "What was that? It felt like it ended up right in my head."

"Mine too," Mike replied.

"That laugh and the marks on the trees that weren't mine can't be a coincidence. Someone or something has deliberately misled us."

As soon as Doug was finished speaking, the laughter came again, but this time it didn't hurt their heads. It just trailed off on the breeze after startling them.

"Creepy," Mike said, looking around for the source of the sound.

"Definitely."

Without warning, a rustling in a tree at the edge of the clearing made them both turn, and a small humanoid flipped majestically off a branch and landed in front of them.

The creature was just under three feet tall and slender. He was dressed in a bright orange one-piece jumpsuit and had a small head, large eyes, and a green-tinged face. "Had you going there, didn't I?"

Without lips to define the pencil thin mouth, it was tough to tell if the creature was smiling or not.

"Who are you ... and what are you?" Mike asked, glancing from Doug to the strange creature.

"I'm Utoov the Keeper, Utoov the Protector. My brother Poov the Great, Poov the Beast Killer and I are the last of our species."

Mike smiled at the names. "Did every one of your species have such grand names?"

Utoov's mouth curled down at the corners in a frown. "I fear you mock me, kind sir."

"Not at all," Mike said and Doug nodded his agreement.

"Are you responsible for the cut marks that have gotten us lost, as well as the creepy laughter?" Doug asked.

Utoov bowed low with a sweeping arm gesture. "The same."

Mike nudged Doug. "If he were fatter, he'd look like a pumpkin, wouldn't he?" he asked.

Doug laughed at the image.

"Ah, now you wound me deeply, even though I know not what this pumpkin may be."

Doug smiled and bowed low. Then trying to mimic the creature's speech pattern, he said, "Begging your pardon, honorable sir. There was no intent to bring offense to you."

Utoov seemed to ponder that statement for a moment then he returned the bow. "Pardon has been granted."

Mike nodded, and taking his cue from Doug, bowed too. "Thank you. If I may ask, why did you mislead us here?"

Utoov crossed his arms. "I fear your follies were many," he said. "It was to save your lives."

Cory took took a deep breath as he stayed just inside the secret door, listening for movement from the corridor. He'd been saved by Poov's actions; of that, he was certain. Especially if Angry Ancient had gotten involved, there'd have been no mercy for him. He was lucky. It sounded, however, as if Poov had not been, and Cory felt genuinely sad over the funny little creature who'd helped him. Remembering that Poov had said this tunnel would lead to his Garlian friends, and hearing nothing from the other side of the door, he slowly wheeled away.

At some point he suspected he would probably reach a tunnel he'd recognize from helping to plot escape plans with his Garlian friends. He kept going until his arms were too tired to continue, but he still didn't know where he was. He felt vulnerable and extremely exposed in the tunnel. Nevertheless he had to stop where he was to rest, and that rest turned into dozing off.

When Cory woke with a start, the sound of footsteps were approaching him from around a bend in the tunnel. Panicked, he wheeled around to look for the source of them, but knew the narrow tunnel had nowhere for him to hide.

"Cory!"

Cory broke into a smile. "Tyncil, You have no idea how good it is to see you."

Tyncil barely managed a smile in return. "Come on, I'll push you," he said. "We have to get out of here. Somehow they know about all of these tunnels now. Someone new must be in charge in the town."

Without any further discussion, Tyncil grabbed the handles of the wheelchair, and off they went. After careening along at a positively frightening speed,

Tyncil finally halted, ran back a few yards, and to Cory's satisfaction, triggered one of the hidden doors to close behind them, giving them some time if they were pursued.

"Nicely done," Cory remarked as Tyncil resumed pushing.

"Thanks to you," Tyncil responded.

"You've seen Brad? Where is he?" Christy asked.

The girl looked at them, seemingly trying to predict how they'd respond to her answer. "He's gone, and Cory isn't here now either."

"Cory?" Christy asked, almost screaming his name in excitement. In the dark, Danny had a tough time following the Garlian's lips. He grabbed Christy's arm impatiently and made his frustration clear.

She signed quickly and turned back to the girl.

"Please, tell me what you know."

The girl nodded then started by introducing herself. "I'm Ufei. Cory spent some time with us, but he's been captured by the Garlians of the town above. They take slaves from us and we try to get them back. Cory helped us greatly to solve a problem we've had since I can remember. Brad met me just where you first saw me. He is ... different, isn't he?"

Christy nodded. "He's actually the best at solving and understanding almost everything we've encountered in this world so far, but yes, he's certainly different."

Danny tried to follow Christy's lips and guess at the other half of the interaction, as it was hard to read the Garlian's lips.

"He will need me ... us—," Danny said, gesturing between himself and Christy, "at some point. His being different also makes it difficult for him to handle certain things. We need to find him."

The girl eyed them for a second. Then she nodded to Danny. "You also are different." It was a statement, not a question. "And you both speak with your hands. I've heard of many who do that far from here in this world, out of necessity. Here there is not the need."

"Please ..." Christy pleaded, impatient for more news or action.

"Follow me, quickly."

They hurried after the girl down the long tunnel. At seemingly arbitrary intervals, Ufei stopped and pressed her hand against the tunnel wall and a door would slide out of a hidden recess. Some doors remained jarred open with a screeching halt; others slid silently, closing off the tunnel behind them. "Cory came up with that strategy and it has worked for us," Ufei finally explained. "It stops any pursuit by those from the town."

Each time they put a door between themselves and possible pursuers, the girl impatiently waved them forward again as she bolted ahead.

When Christy was nearly exhausted and about to ask the girl if they could rest, they came to a spot where two tunnels crossed. To Christy's relief, Ufei stopped at the junction.

"We should be safe here while we wait for my brother, Abei. We have sent a team to try to free Cory." Her voice echoed off the walls in all four directions.

"There was no need," a voice came back in response; it too echoed off the walls and trailed away until it turned into a whisper and was gone. Quickly coming into view from the intersecting tunnel, a male Garlian appeared.

"Abei!" Ufei cried with delight. The two rushed to each other and embraced.

Abei pushed his sister away gently and said, "I've had no chance to speak with you since my rescue, but we must continue and meet up with Tyncil."

As they continued on at a much slower pace this time, Christy said, "You two speak beautiful English."

Ufei explained how they knew English, just as she'd done with Cory, and Christy kept up a stream of signing so Danny was kept in the loop.

Finally they came to a large meeting area off one of the tunnels. The place was filled with Garlians and …

"Cory!" Christy ran to him, and after giving him a hug, hauled off and hit him square in the chest.

"You selfish, arrogant twerp. Because of you, my dad and the detective are God-only-knows where, and my grandfather has disappeared. I can only hope he's still alive. And now Brad's missing too!"

Cory spun away from her and after putting a good length between them, he spun around to face her.

"Nobody asked you to come looking for me, Walker. And that goes for any of you. I've managed ok on my own," Cory said, but Christy's words began to sink in; his face showed it.

"Brad? He's here?"

"What did you think was going to happen? Your mom okay'ed it in order to find you, but Brad wouldn't come back, even for you, without Danny. So that's why he's here too. Without Brad, we'd never have come close to finding you. But Brad split from me and Danny when we weren't looking. We don't know exactly where he is."

Cory was silent and then tears came to his eyes. "The dope. And all for nothing."

"What do you mean, for nothing?" Christy asked.

"I haven't found anything. No more devices. I thought it would be easy."

Cory shook his head, changing the subject back to Brad. "Brad takes off a lot. Mom and I call it his 'walkabouts.' Of course, then she makes me go find him. I guess I'm going to have to find him again."

"I can't understand it though," Christy said, shaking her head. "He wouldn't come back here without Danny so why would he take off without us?"

"When he's in the mood for a 'walkabout,' nobody can stop him. Besides, Danny's here isn't he?"

Danny waved his hands for attention, then said, "Maybe he was just impatient with us and needed to go ahead alone to find you, Cory."

Cory shook his head. "No, it's a 'walkabout' that's for sure."

"Does he ever return on his own, without you finding him?" Christy asked.

"Sure, if he gets distracted long enough by the sight of a butterfly or the way the grass waves in the breeze, or counting a bunch of ants crawling up a tree, the mood might pass him by."

Christy shook her head at Cory's explanation, then turned to Ufei, Abei and Tyncil, and the rest of the Garlians. "You're nothing like the Garlians we saw in an underground city we were lost in."

Cory interrupted before she could continue. "Something funny is going on there. Even the Garlians who held me captive seem upset about that. An old Garlian named Randle implied that someone had messed with those Garlians in the city. And he wants to find out who. Randle is a real nasty dude. Somehow he spent years on Earth and he said it wasn't fun."

"We've heard of this evil that's been done to our kin in the cities. Rumors only though," Ufei replied. "It is depressing to know it's true."

"Oh, and guess what?" Cory continued. "I met Angry Ancient in Boakly and I'm pretty sure he sentenced me to death. And Randle has no love for Angry Ancient either."

"What?" Danny said. "Did I read your lips right?"

Christy replied for Cory. "Yeah, you did."

Danny threw his hands up in the air. "Great, so now we have to deal with Angry Ancient again. So what's the plan?"

"I agree with Cory that we should find Brad first then figure out what to do next."

Cory turned to face Ufei. "Can you guys help us?

Ufei glanced at her companions. "Of course, we will help in any way that we can," she said.

Everyone in the room started to either talk, plan, or listen to the plans of the others when a voice rose above the confusion.

"We don't have to find Cory."

Christy screamed with relief. "Brad!"

CHAPTER 15

"How did tricking us save our lives?" Mike asked Utoov, abandoning the stilted speech they'd been using to play along with the small creature.

"If you'd stepped into the entrance from the clearing, there were a dozen or more Ancients waiting down the tunnel just around the bend. I figured you didn't want to bump into them."

"Why didn't you just show yourself and warn us?" Doug asked.

"What? And miss out on seeing your faces when you couldn't figure out what was going on. Not a chance."

Mike was staring at Utoov closely and after a few seconds he shook his head in confusion. "Utoov, I've been watching your mouth moving. It's not exactly matching up with what you're saying." He turned to Doug. "It's like watching a badly dubbed Japanese movie."

Doug shrugged.

Utoov laughed. "I'm speaking in my own language, but because I'm telepathic, you're hearing English. I have no idea what a Japanese movie is, but I imagine watching my mouth closely would be unsettling."

Doug smiled. "That's why your English sounds so natural I guess."

Mike interrupted. "So we're stuck here? We can't get back through the tunnel that's really a portal to this world?"

Utoov paced the small clearing, scratching away at his circle drawn in the loose dirt. "Yes, the Ancients must by now have set up someone to watch for your return."

The little creature faced Doug and Mike. "You shouldn't go back that way anyway."

"But we have to if we want to find the rest of our group that came here and then get back to our home," Mike said, shaking his head.

"Cory? Is he one of your group?" Utoov asked.

"You've seen Cory?" Doug asked, excitement showing in his voice.

Utoov shook his head. "No, but my brother Poov has met him." Then Utoov became silent and crossed his arms. "My brother and I can communicate over great distances telepathically, but I haven't been able to sense my brother for the last few hours. That worries me. This Cory is a prisoner in Boakly. My brother enjoys popping in and out of the cells where Boakly houses their prisoners. The last that we communicated, Poov was going to free Cory from his imprisonment. I've heard nothing since, though."

"What's Boakly?" Doug asked.

Utoov smiled slightly. "What isn't it? The Ancients built many cities or small communities above the ground. Boakly was one of them, but it was abandoned. Over time, Garlians have constructed primitive buildings on top of that abandoned community; it's a very confusing jumble of structures with many hidden passages back to the underground tunnels that the Ancients loved so well."

Mike looked at Doug. "Maybe we can find Cory and then try to meet up with everyone else."

Doug nodded, then Mike turned to Utoov. "Can you get us to Boakly if we can get out of the underground city?"

"Yes, and it will give me a chance to try to find out why I can't reach my brother. I fear something is terribly wrong."

Mike nodded. "Ok then, but how do we get back if we can't use the portal we came here through?"

Utoov, to their surprise, bent at the knees and then sprung up in the air, doing a backflip and landing on his feet again.

"Ah, I haven't told you my secret yet. We're going back to the pyramid."

"Why? It's guarded. We heard voices coming from it."

Utoov shook his head. "Ah, not really." Then he pointed to a small stone on the ground.

Before Mike or Doug knew it, they heard the same faint chanting they'd heard coming from the pyramid. But this time it was coming from the stone.

Mike grinned despite his irritation. "That was you?"

Utoov bowed. "The same. Telepathy comes in handy. You only thought you heard voices coming from the pyramid. Remember I am called Utoov the Keeper, Utoov the Protector. It is my duty to guard the pyramid."

"But what will that do? How will getting to the pyramid help us get back?" Doug asked, frowning.

"Because," Utoov began, drawing out the suspense by pacing a few steps before continuing, "my pyramid— and I do think of it as mine— holds the secret to everything."

"What do you mean ... *everything*?" Mike asked.

"A bit of background information is in order I think. When the Ancients first learned they were doomed, they did many things to try to prevent it."

Doug interrupted. "We've already dealt with the crippling wind and sound in many areas."

"Yes," Utoov continued. "And of course some of the portals also came out of that need for self-preservation. Sadly, for the most part, nothing was effective for the vast majority of their civilization. But they were great explorers too, and created many portals for that reason alone. They created many different styles of portal, some stationary and linked to bodies of water, some doorways that you have no idea are actually portals till you step through them, and some created wholly by portable devices."

Utoov hesitated, struggling with something internally. "I have no idea what it will translate to in your minds, but I will give an example of what the pyramid contains and hopefully you'll understand."

Utoov sat down before continuing. "The pyramid is massive, you can see that. But like an iceberg, you are seeing only a small portion of the whole. It is many times larger underground than is visible. Essentially, from inside the pyramid, you can get to any destination that they have ever linked to with any of their portals. That was a convenient thing, but a dangerous one too."

"Sort of 'one portal to rule them all,'" Doug offered.

"Not exactly, but close. There are many, many portals in the pyramid. Each portal they've ever created has a corresponding one in the pyramid that is linked to the same destination as its original. So I guess you could say one pyramid to rule them all. 'All' referring to portals, of course. And they didn't build the pyramid— they found it when they opened up the portal to this world. What made them decide to mirror every portal and put their duplicates in the pyramid has been lost to history, I'm afraid. Perhaps they anticipated a time when they would be destroyed, conquered or subjugated as a race. They obviously knew of all these other worlds, since they had portals to them, so it wouldn't be beyond the realm of reason to assume they saw each of the worlds as a possible threat as well as an opportunity. And in fact, their worst fears came to pass, so maybe it was just good planning."

Doug and Mike both sat silent, entirely fascinated by Utoov's story. "And they also put their entire history in there, inside a crystal that is very well hidden, and also on the walls, etched in full color. From their primitive beginnings to the moment they were invaded ... it's all there, magnificently rendered by hundreds of artists over many hundreds of years.

"Though it's probably not as large overall as one of their underground cities, there are rooms upon rooms filled with their technology and vehicles. Basically their whole world as it was, they tried to store a good representation of it in there."

Mike was puzzled after the little humanoid finished. "If they didn't build the pyramid, only found it after creating a portal to this world, and they've filled it with their civilization's artifacts and portals, what happened to what was in it originally? And what happened to the builders?"

"The pyramid was empty and no trace of the builders was ever found. For generations though, there were stories that got passed down about mysterious sightings of fleeting shadows inside the pyramid that the artists and cartographers swore had to be the original builders, or their ghosts. And many things supposedly went missing or moved from place to place without Ancient intervention. Probably those were stories made up to impress or scare. Many a young Ancient was entertained by such bedtime stories."

"That's a treasure of artifacts and knowledge beyond belief," Mike said, breaking a long silence after Utoov's story.

Doug nodded. "Ancients today should have access to the pyramid. It could rebuild their world, I'd think."

Utoov shook his head. "No, I think not."

Mike frowned. "Why not?"

"As long as I'm guarding the pyramid, I won't let that happen."

"You? Why not?" Mike asked again.

Utoov stood silently seething with anger for a moment. "I told you— I am Utoov the Keeper, Utoov the Protector. What I 'keep' is the pyramid out of the hands of the Ancients. What I 'protect' is the universe from those same Ancients."

Doug said, "I don't understand."

"If I gave the impression that I was in favor of that civilization I am sorry. I want them to disappear completely. They aren't a benign race. They may have eventually been conquered and wiped out almost completely, but they were a race who enslaved others most cruelly. They got what they deserved. Believe me when I say that. My race was one of the ones they captured, brought to their world, enslaved, and systematically and slowly wiped out."

"There's no question ... we have to see if we can find out what happened to detective Lockhart and my dad," Christy said as the group gathered around her after Brad's return. They tried to get useful information from him about where he'd gone but he just stood mute, ignoring them, so they moved on to what to do next.

"I can get us to the elevator," Cory offered.

"Will it work?" Christy asked.

"It got me up to that weird moving street. It can probably head down to the city as well as it comes up from it. It sounds like you guys came down here the same way that I did. We can head back to the surface the same way. "

Ufei nodded. "Yes, that is so. I took you all down through the same hidden door."

"Good," Cory said. "Then we use that to get back above ground and I'll get us back to the platform to Zyltruubanik."

Christy looked at Brad as she signed and said, "Ok, sounds like a plan. But we have to get from Zyltruubanik to Abuuenki where we left my dad and Detective Lockhart. Then we'll have to rely on Brad to try and keep us out of trouble while we search for them. And don't forget, Brad swore that Tarynn was lying to us about where Cory went, which we now know is true. Let's hope we can use the portal in Zyltruubanik without any interference from that computer."

Cory looked as if he was about to respond when a Garlian who Christy didn't know burst into the room, waving. Ufei went over to him. He looked grim. The two whispered together for a few seconds, then Ufei nodded, concern showing on her face as she clapped her hands together for attention.

"We have to flee. There are armed Garlians and Ancients swarming through the tunnels, breaking their way through the closed doors we activated to slow them down. They have already slain two who were unfortunate enough to be in their way."

Christy signed to Danny to explain what Ufei had said, and Danny shook his head, saying bitterly, "This has to be Angry Ancient's doing."

Cory nodded. "And Randle's too," he said. "We better get out of here fast."

"Everyone follow me," Ufei commanded loudly. "There's a back way up to the surface that I hope they still haven't found out about. It's our only chance if they're hunting through the tunnels."

Christy smiled at and declined the help of a Garlian who attempted to push Cory's chair as they all filed out. She grabbed the handles of his wheelchair and they joined the procession.

Cory called to his brother once they were all on the move: "Brad! Stay with Christy and me. Don't wander off."

They followed Ufei through a dimly lit tunnel, which was just light enough that they didn't have to stop to put any crystals in to light their way. Christy also noticed they didn't stop and trigger any doors to try and delay their pursuers. Time was more important now, it seemed.

Within ten minutes of leaving the meeting room, they came to a steep staircase.

"Up here," Ufei said pointing, and several of the Garlians sprinted up without looking back.

Ufei barked orders, taking care that Cory was accounted for.

"You, you, and you," she pointed, "help Cory out of the chair." Then she pointed at two other Garlians. "You link hands and carry him up. Quickly." The Garlians did as she directed and soon Cory was resting between two Garlians with their hands linked under him like a chair seat and he had his arms wrapped around their shoulders. The Garlians were small in stature but had surprising strength.

"Halfway up, you two take over," Ufei said, pointing again.

Christy removed the platform Cory's dad had made for him and then collapsed his chair. Cory twisted around as he was being carried up the stairs. "Brad, come on, hurry up." Seeing Danny about to grab the platform from Christy, he yelled, "Just leave it."

Danny nodded and he and Christy hefted the wheelchair between them and started up the stairs, following everyone else.

Carrying Cory's wheelchair between them, the flight of stairs was long and exhausting for Christy and Danny. But Christy knew that the Garlians taking turns carrying Cory up the stairs had a more difficult time of it.

Like a swarm of ants, they all poured out of the staircase entrance into daylight above ground.

Ufei waited until they all were up and Cory had been put back in his chair. She nodded thank you's to the Garlians who had carried him, then she pointed. "That way."

"That is not safe, and you know it!" one of the Garlians protested loudly.

Ufei turned to face him. "It's that direction or none!" she yelled. "Now let's go."

Christy scanned the landscape in all directions and immediately understood what the conflict was. Ufei had pointed to the only direction that had the broken remnants of a beltway. Any other direction and Cory's wheelchair would quickly get bogged down. With Cory in tow, there was only one way they could go.

"Ufei, take your friends and go wherever it's safest. Danny, Brad and I can manage Cory's chair. We have to follow the beltway to get back to Zyltruubanik."

"No, we are together and that is how we will stay."

Before Christy or any of the Garlians could argue, Ufei was off at a run.

CHAPTER 16

It quickly became apparent to Christy that they were not on the same beltway they'd been on before. "Do you think this goes back to the platform?" Christy asked breathlessly as she pushed Cory's wheelchair. Danny and the Garlians kept pace with them. "It's not the beltway I traveled on to get to the outskirts of Boakly, so I don't know," Cory said. After a few minutes of silence he added, "This whole beltway is down. Most sections of what I traveled on were working fine, even if they were in really bad shape."

Ufei heard the question and paced herself to run in-line with Christy. "Yes, this section of broken road will come back to Zyltruubanik," she said. The

Garlian girl hesitated, then seemed to think better of continuing.

"What?" Christy asked. Christy thought the girl seemed fearful of something, but it was difficult to tell what the Garlians were thinking, with their tiny eyes and differently shaped faces.

"Nothing," Ufei said unconvincingly. Then she added, "But we do have to abandon this road and travel across more difficult terrain before we get to the platform that Cory speaks of."

Christy stared for a second at Ufei and the girl stared back, only for a second, as they hit a particularly bad section littered and pockmarked so badly that they had to keep their focus on their careful footwork.

Soon that agonizingly slow progress was the norm, as they were forced to stop repeatedly and remove things in their path to continue forward.

After nearly two hours of such slow progress, Ufei waved for everyone's attention.

"I think we can stop here to rest for a bit."

Danny and Brad immediately slumped onto the cracked remains of the beltway surface. Christy sat down next to them and closed her eyes. She had pushed the wheelchair the whole time, only able to do so because of the slow pace of progress.

Most of the Garlians were also sitting and resting, but Ufei was still on her feet, talking to some of the other Garlians. She seemed to be encouraging them, until an exchange grew heated. Christy opened her eyes at the noise. Ufei was having angry words with the same Garlian who'd called her out about heading in a risky direction to accommodate Cory's wheelchair.

After the argument ended, Ufei came over to Christy's group. "What was that about?" Christy asked quietly.

"Difference of opinion only. Nothing to be alarmed about," she said, dismissing the altercation with a wave. "We have come to the end of our roadway. As difficult as it has been, without it, travel will be worse. We may have to take turns carrying you, Cory. We will share that task and also the task of carrying your chair. I see no other way."

Brad had been sitting quietly next to Danny while Ufei spoke. Suddenly he sprung up and bounded off of the crumbling roadway, heading to the remnants of a small cluster of low buildings, in even worse shape than the beltway. They'd been passing similar ruins regularly but after the first few, nobody gave them any thought.

"Brad, what are you doing? Come back here!" Cory yelled.

Brad ignored him. Danny watched Brad, then watched Cory shouting, and sighed audibly, getting up reluctantly to follow. Christy stood up. "I'll go too and see what he's up to," she said to Cory.

Christy quickly caught up to Danny, who nodded at her as they approached Brad. Danny tapped Brad on the sleeve and signed at him. Brad made a few quick signing responses and continued on, disappearing behind a crumbling foundation, overrun with weeds and moss.

Danny was about to go after him but Christy held him back. "What did he say? He signed too fast for me," she said.

Danny shrugged. "He's looking for a road for Cory."

"I imagine no race of people is completely without its skeletons in the closet," Mike said, responding to Utoov's revelation that his species had been brought to the Empty World as slaves and faced genocide at the hands of the Ancients.

Doug nodded. "How did you become the Keeper and the Protector?" he asked.

"When the Cleaners came in to conquer the Ancients, the remainder of my people went into hiding. After the war that ensued, we realized that the Ancients' civilization, and that of the Cleaners left to govern them, were regressing into primitive societies. We knew that they didn't remember what their forbearers had stored in the pyramid or anything about the portals still on their world. It was an opportunity for us to survive without further persecution and to keep any knowledge of how to rebuild their civilization from them."

"So," Doug began, "you've taken over or had the task passed down to you?"

Utoov shook his tiny head. "No, I've been the only one from the beginning."

Mike and Doug stared at Utoov in disbelief.

"We need to stop wasting time and get to the pyramid, but it's true, I am old. Really old by your standards."

Mike and Doug looked at each other, then Mike gestured to Utoov. "Lead on, oh ancient one."

Utoov stared at him and Mike smiled. "Sorry, bad choice of words."

"Yah think?" Utoov growled as he started off.

Utoov didn't follow the path that he'd marked to trick Doug, but they got to the side of the pyramid just the same. The little humanoid broke out of the lush growth and into the clearing around the pyramid before the others. He waited until Mike and Doug caught up, then they sat down together and rested for a few minutes. The humid tropical air made their clothing cling and small insects buzzed annoyingly around their heads. Even Utoov seemed bothered by the combination of heat and insects.

After swatting away some buzzing insect that looked like a large fly, Utoov stood up. "Let's go, time's a-wasting."

As Mike and Doug stood, ready to go on, they heard shouting from farther ahead, coming from another side of the pyramid that was hidden from view. It sounded like Ancient to Mike, but he couldn't be sure.

Just then, Utoov squealed something under his breath and bolted back the way they'd come, disappearing into the jungle.

"Coward," Doug said. "You'd think he would—"

Doug didn't get the chance to finish his comment. From around the corner, a dozen Ancients appeared, spears raised and pointing directly at them, too close to make a break for it.

"Oh boy," Doug said, his shoulders slumping in resignation.

Christy and Danny followed Brad into the ruined foundation. When they got inside, Brad was already pulling up plants by the roots and tossing them behind him. Having witnessed the brilliance of his seemingly nonsensical actions in the past, they just stood quietly and watched.

After grunting as he uprooted a handful of weeds, Brad absentmindedly flung them over his shoulder to land at Christy's feet. Then he knelt down and began digging into the disturbed dirt. Christy and Danny watched as he brushed the dirt off of something. He gripped it and pulled, grunting again. Finally Brad turned, his eyes pleading with the two of them. Christy shrugged and Danny threw his hands up, but both rushed forward to help.

Brad had a grip on the edge of something, straining to free it from the surrounding earth, and when they knelt down beside him, they realized the object Brad was pulling on was a sheet of metal about a quarter of an inch think. With the three of them pulling, the metal sheet slid out from under years of dirt and debris.

It took a couple of minutes, but finally the three of them had a four foot by six or seven foot sheet of thin metal that was as light as cardboard. Danny easily lifted it by himself.

Once the sheet was free and Danny was brushing it clear of dirt, Brad stood, spun around, and hopped over a mound of dirt, beginning the process again.

After they had another sheet of metal uncovered and stacked atop the first one, Christy tapped Brad on the shoulder and asked, "How did you know these were here?" She'd already figured out their usefulness to them but hadn't a clue as to how he'd known to search for them buried in the dirt.

Brad pointed to the foundation wall before he yanked the two sheets away from the surprised Danny. Without so much as a 'thanks,' he darted off to join the group that was waiting patiently with puzzled expressions on their Garlian faces.

Christy and Danny quickly followed.

Brad had already laid down one of the sheets over the spongy ground and handed the second one to a startled Garlian who stood staring at it like it was poisonous.

Christy quickly explained, pointing at the Garlian holding the second sheet. "Set that down on the end of the first one. Cory, you wheel over the platform. Then," she said, pointing to a small group of Garlians, "one of you pick it up when he's started onto the second one and quickly lay it down in front. If we keep doing that, we should be able to make much better time than if we carry Cory and his wheelchair."

The Garlians nodded enthusiastically as they realized that there was an answer to Cory's wheelchair sinking down into the soft moss.

As they got going again, and the process proved to be working marvelously, Ufei stepped back and matched her pace with Christy's.

"He's got a lot of hidden talents, doesn't he?" Ufei asked, nodding toward Brad.

Christy grinned. "We find more of them every day."

"Do you recognize any of these jokers?" Mike asked Doug. As captives of the Ancients, they were tied up and prodded to march out.

Doug scanned the group surrounding them as they walked.

"Yeah, the Ancient with the mostly missing ear. He was with TuMaz-Tan when Trevor and I were captured before. Trevor called him One-Ear. A couple of the others look vaguely familiar too."

"So this is probably TuMaz-Tan's doing," Mike guessed, eliciting a slap across the back of the head and an angry stream of words from one of their captors for his troubles.

Mike and Doug looked at each other, silently agreeing to keep their conversations to a minimum.

Under the direction of One-Ear, the group followed the same path that Doug had marked. Prodded viciously by One-ear, the group pushed it hard. It didn't take nearly as long to return to the portal disguised as a tunnel exit as it had taken Mike and Doug to get to the pyramid. After entering the portal and traversing the long tunnel, they found themselves assembled in a large room somewhere in Abuuenki. They were exhausted, sweaty and insect-bitten.

One-Ear grunted something in Ancient and motioned to them to sit down. The relative cool of the underground city was a stark contrast to the heat and humidity of the jungle world, and was a relief which even the Ancients appeared grateful for.

After resting for a few minutes, the Ancients began talking amongst themselves, so Mike chanced to speak quietly with Doug.

"Doug, it seems they knew all about the pyramid and the portal to get to it."

Doug hesitated before answering, waiting to see if Mike's comment would spur any repercussions. When it didn't, he nodded and said, "Yeah, and they knew exactly where the mechanisms were to spring the doors open. Those took us a while to find."

"It makes me wonder how effective Utoov's guarding of the pyramid has been," Mike replied.

Doug leaned in closer. "Maybe TuMaz-Tan and his gang are the only Ancients who know about it."

"I wouldn't put it past that conniving Ancient to keep what's in there to himself till he can profit from it somehow. He clearly has proven that he wants to wipe out the race of Cleaners and set himself up as the leader of the Ancients. If Utoov is telling the truth about what's in that pyramid, TuMaz-Tan could definitely use it to his advantage."

Suddenly, one of the Ancients barked out orders and the rest stopped talking. They stood up and waited. One-Ear pointed and prompted one of the others to poke Mike and Doug until they got up too. When One-Ear pointed again, another Ancient walked toward them, waving a menacing knife. Mike and Doug could only stand there as he approached them. To their relief, he stepped behind them and with a couple of swift downward thrusts, sliced through their bonds. Then One-Ear barked orders again and all the Ancients bowed at the waist, extending their arms out just as another Ancient entered the room. The Ancient who'd cut their bonds slapped them both on the back of the head and they were forced to mirror the actions of the Ancients.

Mike lifted his eyes to see who they all were bowing to. It was TuMaz-Tan.

CHAPTER 17

As Christy and Danny walked alongside Cory and the Garlians, they were amused at how enthusiastically the two Garlians picking up and repositioning the sheets of metal were performing their task.

Christy tapped Danny to get his attention. "How did Brad know to look for those?" she asked, signing.

Danny smiled. "Brad's been staring at all the ruins we've passed along this route and a few of the foundations had metal frames sticking up. My guess is he probably figured that those metal frames had metal walls slid into them in the past. Or maybe we even passed a foundation with a panel or two still attached.

Even if we didn't notice, Brad would have. That's what the sheets are, I think; they're wall panels that they built those buildings with."

As Christy and Danny were signing back and forth, Cory suddenly stopped and spun his chair around, staring out toward the landscape and its crumbling ruins that had remained a constant for most of their travels. The group of Garlians clustered around Cory's wheelchair halted. Christy and Danny stopped too, and Danny grabbed Brad and prevented him from walking off without them. Brad pulled out of Danny's grasp but stayed put.

"I think this is close to where the platform I came up on was. But we're approaching from a different direction, so I'm not sure."

"Should some of us fan out and search for it?" Christy asked.

"Yeah, thanks," Cory said, pointing to a section off to their left. "Start there. That looks the most familiar."

"What are we looking for?" Christy asked.

"A small, square, gray building, one story high. The door will be partway opened. It got stuck when I tried to get off the platform. Hopefully the platform will still be there. If it's gone back down into the city, I don't know what we'll do."

Danny, who'd been watching Cory's lips, said, "I do. We'll hope that Brad can find a stairway down into the city."

Christy smiled. "Plan B."

"Also if you come across some dark greasy stains on the patches of pavement, let me know," Cory said. "I disturbed some creepy spiders, and the disgusting things swarmed up from a crack in the ground and took off. They left a path of nasty behind them and I followed that to the moving beltway. So if you see it, we might be able to follow it in reverse to the platform."

When Cory had finished, some of the Garlians began whispering amongst themselves. Ufei shot them a glare and they fell silent.

"What was that about?" Christy asked. "They're not thrilled with our plan?"

"Nothing," Ufei said, still glaring at some of her group. After turning away to confer with her brother and Tyncil, she said, "The three of us will search too." The skittish Garlians avoided making eye contact as she shot another glare at them.

Christy was curious about the exchange but had to trust Ufei. "Tyncil and I will head directly to where Cory pointed," Christy said to Ufei. "If you want to take Abei and head there," she said, pointing in the opposite direction, "then Danny and Brad can search the area between."

Before anyone could start searching, the skittish Garlians started whining as a soft rustling noise began to grow louder.

"Look!" Cory said, pointing.

Rising out of cracks in the ground in every direction was a swarming mass of black spiders, each easily as large as the largest tarantula that Christy had ever seen.

Murray sprang up into Cory's lap, hissing, his hair standing straight up on his back.

Ufei turned to Christy. "They are poisonous. We must avoid them at all costs."

As soon as Ufei finished her warning, Brad grabbed Cory's wheelchair handles and began pushing, picking his way across sections of pavement that were free of spiders.

Christy wasn't surprised that Brad was taking charge in his own way, and she yelled to everyone to follow him.

When some of the Garlians continued to stand around, whining and covering their eyes, Christy turned and yelled again.

"If you want to get out of here alive, let's go now!"

Ufei also yelled something in her own language at the others and they finally started after Brad.

Brad threaded between swarms of spiders on either side of them with apparent ease. The spiders seemed to have set patterns, and fortunately did not break those patterns to attack any of the group as they followed Brad and Cory. After a few minutes, Christy began to see the pattern that Brad was using to guide them. The ruined pavement had very distinct dark stains, some nearly invisible and some still glistening like shiny oil slicks from the spiders. Brad was keeping away from any of the stains, old or new, as he picked his way along.

As the swarms of spiders grew, birds the size of large hawks began to swoop down from the trees all around them, plucking spiders with their sharp talons and tossing them high into the air. As the spiders came down again, the birds caught them in their beaks and swallowed them in one gulp. Despite the attacks by the birds, there weren't nearly enough of them to stem the tide of the swarms.

One of the Garlians who'd caught up to Brad stumbled momentarily and stuck his hands out to break his fall. A fresh slick of residue from some recent swarm coated his hands. When he got up and brushed his hands on his thighs to wipe the slimy oil off, a swarm of spiders immediately poured out of one of the cracks and began to climb up his legs.

The Garlian screamed, swatting at the first few spiders, but they continued to crawl over his body. Everyone came to a stop, the horror of the Garlian's predicament on their faces.

Danny was the first to spring to the poor Garlian's aid. He started grabbing the spiders and flinging them away as fast and as far as he could. The Garlian's eyes, although terrified, also showed gratitude as he and Danny worked in unison to get rid of the poisonous creatures.

It wasn't going to be enough and Christy saw that, but if she tried to help, she'd only get in the way. The swarm of spiders seemed endless. As soon as Danny and the Garlian could pick a few spiders off, more were waiting to take their place. It was just a matter of time before one of them was struck with the poisonous venom.

All of a sudden, Murray leaped off Cory's lap. He was an orange blur, hissing and swatting with his claws— not at the spiders already on the Garlian, but at the ones still swarming and waiting their turn to attack. It only took a few second for the tide to turn in the Garlian's favor. Soon the spiders redirected themselves away from the Garlian and headed off in another direction. Murray calmly jumped back into Cory's lap and settled down again. Danny was flinging the last spider off of the Garlian when he grabbed his own wrist. "Ouch!"

"Danny!" Christy screamed.

Abei was already springing into action. He tore a long strip of his clothing and tied it quickly around Danny's bicep, pulling the half knot tight and holding it down with two fingers. To everyone watching, he shouted, "Somebody find me a short stick!"

Christy knew what Abei was doing and had already slipped her arms out of her pack. A second after Abei's command, she handed him a pen. Abei replaced his fingers with the pen and loosened the half knot underneath it slightly, then tied a full knot on top of it, completing his hasty tourniquet. He twisted the pen parallel to Danny's arm, tightening it again, then motioned for Christy to hold it. He tore another shorter strip of clothing while Christy kept the pen secure, and wrapped it around Danny's arm and over the pen, tying it so it wouldn't untwist. Danny winced slightly but otherwise took things well.

"We have to loosen that every few minutes, but loss of circulation in his arm is the least of our worries," Abei explained quickly. "He will shortly pass out despite how quickly I applied the tourniquet, and he needs an antidote to the poison as soon as possible."

Christy stared at the grim-faced Garlian, and the look she got in return told her that their prospects of an antidote were slim.

As if on cue, Danny staggered and stumbled into Cory's chair. Abei caught him, letting him slide gently to the ground.

Cory wheeled his chair back a step and pushed Murray off. "Here, lift him onto my lap," he said. "I'll hold onto him."

Abei and Tyncil picked Danny up and positioned him on Cory's lap. Cory held Danny around the waist. As his head flopped back onto Cory's shoulder, Danny groaned.

After loosening and tightening the tourniquet, Abei stood up straight, looking grim. "He won't last long, a day at most."

Brad began to pace in the narrow confines of a clear spot on the pavement. He took off the light sweater he had on and leapt over a four foot wide stain the spiders had left.

Ufei looked at Christy quizzically, but Christy just shrugged. "There has to be a reason," she said.

"But this is no time for whatever he's up to," Abei cautioned.

"Do you have an antidote? Can you get one quickly?" Christy asked.

Abei stared at her, a helpless stare that told her the answer. He answered anyway. "Any antidote we have is back below the streets of Boakly."

Danny groaned again.

"He will be completely unconscious soon, not just semi-conscious," Abei continued.

"Then we have to see what Brad's up to," Christy said, biting her lip.

Brad was jumping over some of the spiders that were still swarming, avoiding them by staying on clear areas. Without warning, he cut through a wide swath of spiders moving as a single entity. He kicked many up into the air and squashed others underfoot as he ran. The hawk-like birds swooped all around him, plucking the kicked spiders from mid-air.

Cory craned his neck around Danny's head to watch his brother. "What's he doing?"

"I don't know, but I'm sure there's a reason for it," Christy replied.

When Brad reached a small cluster of trees, he stopped running and began screaming and waving his sweater high over his head. From the trees in front of him, several of the birds took flight, screeching their displeasure. Brad immediately stooped down and picked something up, hurling it into the nearest tree. When nothing happened, Brad circled around again, scanning the ground before picking up something else. He tried hurling it at the tree again, and this time, a nest came tumbling down. Brad was quick. He caught the nest before it hit the ground. Clutching it close, he started back toward everyone.

Within minutes, he had poked a hole in an egg with his finger and was kneeling down with it in front of Danny. Putting the egg up to Danny's lips, he stopped to look at Christy for a second. "Danny will get better," he said.

Danny groaned again. "Brad," Christy began, "do you want me to get Danny to drink that egg?"

For a flickering second, Brad made eye contact again. That was all Christy needed. She took the egg from Brad and stroked Danny's cheek. "Danny, can you hear me?" she asked. "I need you to drink this. Please."

Danny's mouth parted slightly and his eyes fluttered once.

Christy put the egg right up to his mouth. With her finger she broke the shell some more and let the fluid inside dribble into his mouth. For a second it seemed he wouldn't respond, but then she saw him swallow and swallow again until the shell was empty.

"Again," Brad said, handing Christy another egg. Christy repeated the process and after she tossed the empty shell, she turned to look at Brad. "Danny's better," he said.

Despite Brad's statement, Danny certainly didn't look any better.

"The city," Brad announced as he bolted off.

Abei reached and grabbed Christy's arm. "Stop him, quickly!"

Christy was about to question why, but seeing the concern on Abei's face, she just yelled to Brad's receding form. "Brad, come back! Come back, please."

Brad hesitated and Christy yelled again. "Stop, we need to talk. Come back here."

Realizing that nobody was following, Brad turned around and started back.

"The city," Brad said as he joined then again.

Christy turned to Abei and nodded, giving him the chance to explain.

Abei gestured at Danny. "I think what Brad did may boost Danny's immune system. It was pretty ingenious of him. Clearly the birds have built up immunity to the spider bites over the millennia they've been preying on them for food. Those eggs must carry a powerful dose of that immunity."

A deep intake of breath interrupted Abei. It was Danny. He moaned and opened his eyes.

"Danny!" Christy leaned over and hugged him.

"I don't feel so good," Danny said in a weak voice.

Christy stood up and grabbed Brad. Despite his best efforts, Brad couldn't squirm out of Christy's bear hug. "Brad, thank you!" Christy said tearfully. "I don't know how you knew what to do, but you did it." She let Brad go and he moved away from her.

"Danny is better."

"Yes, Brad, Danny is better," Christy replied, wiping her eyes.

"Ok," Cory said. "Let's get going. Flying fingers, you better recover quickly; you're heavy."

Even the Garlians laughed.

After a moment, Abei cleared his throat for attention. "I'm not through explaining: Danny isn't going to recover just by drinking those eggs. They seem to have helped him fight the poison but they're not an antidote. When you get a disease, you won't be cured by getting the vaccination for that disease. I'm afraid that the antibodies in those eggs are probably acting like a vaccination. It may give immunity to those who haven't been bitten, but it won't act as an antidote and neutralize the poison already in his system."

Christy exhaled loudly. "So we still need the antidote?"

Abei nodded. "I'm afraid so. Brad may have bought him more time but how much is uncertain."

Christy began pacing. "What are we going to do? This is all just too much! First my dad and Detective Lockhart, then Grandpa Jack, and now Danny too? I can't handle this," Christy said, her voice cracking as she choked down a sob.

With her head buried in her hands, Christy's whole body began to shake as she sat on the ground and cried.

Brad stepped closer, knelt down beside Christy and awkwardly lifted his arms, forming a circle just over her head as if he was measuring her circumference.

Then he slipped them around her shoulders and leaned his head against hers.

Cory's jaw fell open. "Whoa, you got a Brad hug! That's quite the rare event, Walker," he said. "So I get to share my chair with flying fingers for a bit longer, huh?"

Christy lifted her head, disturbing Brad who released her from the hug as he leaned backwards.

Through sniffles, she said, "We need a new plan."

Chapter 18

TuMaz-Tan had taken over the duty of barking orders from One-Ear. Mike and Doug were left with no recourse but to try and interpret the actions of everyone around them. From his short stint in captivity, Doug had picked up a few words of Ancient, but they were woefully inadequate to even begin to understand TuMaz.

After he'd ordered their hands to be tied behind their backs again, TuMaz-Tan stepped over, barked unfamiliar words at them, and then struck each of them across the face. After TuMaz's show of dominance, the group of Ancients all sat down again. After one of them yanked on Mike and Doug's shirts, they too were seated.

TuMaz-Tan motioned to One-Ear and the two of them conversed in the corner, away from the rest of the group. As the other Ancients began quietly talking amongst themselves, Mike and Doug looked over at each other but didn't dare speak. As they sat there, a small pebble dropped onto Doug's head. Mike glanced around to see if any of the Ancients had seen it, but none were paying attention. Shifting their gazes upward, they saw Utoov clinging to one of the ceiling beams. He put his finger to his lipless mouth, urging silence.

Doug smiled slightly, then looked down, chancing a quick whisper to Mike. "He followed us."

Any chance for further conversation was ended as TuMaz-Tan came storming over to them and berated them with a stream of foreign words. Realizing that they couldn't understand him, he said in clear English, "You die."

'We've come all this way only to have to turn around and go back to the tunnels under Boakly," Christy lamented.

Abei nodded. "I see no other way if we want to get an antidote into Danny before it's too late."

Brad wrung his hands together. "Brad can help," he said. Traversing over remnants of the swarming spiders, he bolted off toward the distant trees.

Abei turned to Christy who shook her head. "Maybe he's getting more eggs," Christy offered. "It might help."

"Time is critical," Abei replied, but there was nothing anyone could do but wait for Brad to come back.

It seemed like an agonizingly long time before Brad returned cradling a nest and three eggs.

"Let's get going," Christy ordered as soon as he rejoined the group. She grabbed the handles of the wheelchair and began to push Cory and Danny in it.

Having just come from the tunnels, they knew exactly where to go. The going, though no harder than before, seemed more difficult because of the urgency. Christy only hoped that with the help Brad had provided, Danny's body would be able to fight off the poison until they could get him the antidote.

As they were traveling back over one of the stretches they'd needed the sheets of metal for, Danny began to moan again.

Abei went to him and gently checked his forehead. "That is a good sign."

"What is?" Christy asked.

"He is neither too hot nor too cold. As the poison does its damage, he will get increasingly hot, but near the end, deathly cold."

Christy wasn't sure that she wanted to know the signs that might signal the imminent death of her friend, but she nodded anyway.

As familiar as the landscape was, its crumbling concrete, deep cracks and infirm ground all took a toll on everyone's patience. Several times, the moans coming from Danny seemed to urge them to greater speed only to have their path mock them.

There was no resting; it was as if an unspoken agreement kept them moving forward, pushing beyond fatigue. Suddenly from behind, they heard a lone small voice shouting at them.

Christy heard it and stopped, turning. "What's that?"

"Poov!" Cory yelled. "No, wait— that's not Poov," he said, squinting.

The little humanoid jogged up to the group. "Cory, I have heard of you," he said. "Do you know what has happened to my brother? I cannot contact him. I'm Utoov the Keeper, Utoov the Protector."

Cory hesitated.

"I was afraid of that," Utoov said, his slim shoulders sagging in grief. "Your silence answers for you." After a moment, Utoov addressed the group. "I have come from the city underground called Abuuenki," he said.

Christy cried out, "My dad!"

Utoov nodded. "The ones called Mike and Doug are in great danger. They have been captured and are to die. I don't know when, but I imagine the time left to them is short."

"No!" Christy screamed.

Abei reached over again, feeling Danny's forehead. "He is getting hot." Christy groaned in response, burying her face in her hands.

Ufei, seeing Christy's near helplessness, said, "Tyncil, you, Christy and the rest of our group will go with Utoov to rescue the humans. Abei, you and I will get Danny to our home under Boakly for the antidote."

"No, I can't abandon Danny no matter what," Christy said, her face still buried. "Ufei, please ... you and Tyncil follow Utoov with the rest of your group. I trust you to help my dad and the detective if it's at all possible."

Ufei nodded. "Done." Ufei spoke to her companions then turned to Abei, embracing him. "Our reunion has been short but we will meet again once we have finished the tasks we have been given."

"Go in health," Abei said. Then he turned to Christy and said, "We are running out of time."

Christy nodded, stood up, and addressed Utoov. "Thank you," she said. "I hope you are in time to save them."

Utoov bowed. "It seems all of us have the same issue now, and that is time. Let us depart."

Both groups started again almost immediately in opposite directions. Within minutes, when she turned around, Christy could no longer see Ufei's group.

Mike nudged Doug from his spot next to him on the floor. "I don't want to go out like a couple of lambs led to slaughter. How about you?" he asked.

"Agreed," Doug said, nodding.

"I think we're safe for the moment. Everyone is either getting ready to sleep or already sleeping. We'll probably be killed as soon as they wake up, or be led somewhere else to be killed. Neither thought is appealing. We need to try and get away now, as soon as everyone is asleep."

"I'm sure someone will remain awake," Doug whispered.

"True. We probably won't have more than a few seconds after we make a break for it before everyone will be awake again and coming after us."

"I don't like our chances with our hands tied behind our backs," Doug replied.

"That's why the first thing we do is grab for that knife." Mike nodded his head toward an Ancient close by who was already sleeping, a knife sheathed on his belt.

Doug smiled. "I'll try to slide over slowly until it's in reach. If I can cut myself free unnoticed, then do the same for you, our run out of here just might work."

"If we make it to the door, let's head straight to the portal to the jungle world and the pyramid. If what Utoov says is true, the pyramid might be our best option."

Agonizingly slow, Doug was already sliding, back first, toward the sleeping Ancient to reach the knife with his tied hands. Several times, Doug had to stop as some Ancient or another stirred, only to resume inching closer to the knife when he felt it was safe.

It took a long time, but finally Doug felt the knife under his fingers. Inch by inch, without the benefit of sight, he slipped the knife slowly from its sheath. Then came the awkward process of grasping the knife in his tied hands and sawing at his bonds. Several minutes after starting on his bonds, his hands broke free. Keeping his hands behind him, Doug slipped the knife under his shirt, tucking the hilt into his belt. Then he gathered up the cut rope, stuffed that into his pants, and started the slow crawl back toward Mike while keeping up the appearance of his hands still being tied behind his back.

When he was beside Mike again, Doug withdrew the knife and began sawing through his bonds. It didn't take quite as long since Doug's hands were free. When Mike tapped Doug's hand signaling that his own hands were free, Doug again hid the knife under his shirt.

They were looking around, trying to decide when to make a run for it when that decision was abruptly made for them. The sleeping Ancient who Doug had taken the knife from grunted and sat up, startled. Maybe he checked for his knife every so often while he was half asleep, only to drift back once he was assured it was still there. This time it wasn't.

Yelling something to rouse his mates, the Ancient started to stand.

"Now!" Doug whispered, jumping up and grabbing the knife out of his belt. Mike was right with him. Leaping over some and pushing others aside as they bolted for the door, the sounds of sleepy Ancients filled the room. They'd almost made it to the door when two Ancients staggered to their feet and blocked their path. Mike swung at one, hitting him squarely on his elongated jaw. Doug slashed with the knife at the other and was rewarded with a cry of pain as that Ancient staggered back. Their way was clear.

The non-moving beltway they were currently picking their way over was more damaged and decayed than most, making their progress back to Boakly slower than they'd yet experienced. With each moan from Danny, Christy became increasingly anxious and desperate.

Abei checked Danny's forehead repeatedly, sometimes stating what he found, other times, just looking grim and shaking his head. Twice they stopped as Brad handed Christy another egg and she coaxed it down Danny's throat. Whether the eggs helped or not, Danny was still running out of time.

When they entered a more open landscape with slim trees spaced far apart on either side of the beltway, Cory held up his hand for Christy to stop pushing.

"We're not far now, I think. But we're heading toward the entrance we used to escape the Ancients and Garlians, not the one that Ufei took me down the first time," Cory said.

"Yes, we should be in time. As long as we get to the entrance of the tunnels under Boakly quickly," Abei said, again checking Danny's forehead.

They pushed on, Christy feeling more optimistic after Abei's comment. After a few minutes, Abei held up his hand.

"Stop."

"Why?" Christy asked, frowning.

"Look," Abei said, pointing ahead.

Wisps of something, steam or smoke, were rising up out of a few of the cracks in the flexible pavement of the beltway. The same type of wisps were drifting up around the trees beyond the beltway where minutes before, there had been none.

"What is that?" Christy asked.

"We have a problem, I'm afraid." Abei looked grim. "That is no harmless mist. It is a living entity, and it's deadly if it chooses to be."

Christy suddenly remembered seeing the mist before, during her time with Cory before he broke his back. "I've seen this mist before but it seemed to run from me. Cory had wandered away from me and it was getting dark, and I remember thinking that it looked as if it were alive."

"It chose not to attack you. You were very fortunate. It's not really mist though; it's millions of tiny, translucent insects that swarm as one. Their bites are deadly."

Danny moaned again. "We can't stop. We have to go through, even with that deadly swarm," Christy said.

Abei raised nearly non-existent eyebrows. "We will go forward and see what it will do. But if it comes toward us, we have to retreat."

Tentatively, they pushed forward. Almost immediately a swarm poured from the nearest crack, swirling and coalescing before heading in their direction.

"Ah, no!" Christy cried as she spun Cory's chair around and led the retreat away from the swarm.

Once they were out of immediate danger, Christy felt Danny's head. "He's burning up," she announced.

Abei nodded. "Soon he will begin to feel cold, and it will be too late."

"Then I have to push Cory's chair through no matter what, because he'll die here for sure."

CHAPTER 19

Hours after breaking free of the Ancients, Mike and Doug were still running. Fortunately they had much longer legs than the Ancients and they quickly outdistanced them. When they finally broke into the clearing around the pyramid, they were well ahead of their pursuit.

Pausing quickly to catch their breath, Mike asked, "Ready, Doug?"

"Let's go and see what Utoov was talking about."

The entrance was in the shadows, more inviting because of their long run through the jungle than it might have been otherwise. Doug stopped just inside as the shadows deepened, and rummaged for his flashlight. Switching it on and training the light into the gloom, they moved deeper in.

"Hey, shut that off, it hurts my sensitive eyes."

"Utoov!" Doug started. "How did you get here?"

"I met up with your companions and a bunch Garlians. I told them you were about to be killed so they split up. A few of the Garlians came with me to rescue you, but to our surprise, you were gone and the Ancients who'd captured you were in hot pursuit. So that left the portal in Abuuenki unguarded. It would be a poor Keeper who couldn't get back to his Keep through the linking portal in Abuuenki. The Garlians headed back to meet up with their friends."

"The kids are ok?" Doug asked.

"More or less. The younger one— Danny, I think— is sick. They were taking him to Boakly. I recognized the name as that of a small city above-ground. You'd refer to it as a town."

"Will he be ok?"

Utoov hesitated. "I think so," he replied. "They seemed to have things well in hand."

"What do we do now?" Mike began. "With you here, we will defer to you. It's your Keep."

Utoov stepped to the smooth stone wall and did something they could not see. Light flooded the hallway ahead. "Follow me."

"But what about the Ancients following us?" Mike asked.

Utoov smiled. "They will never get inside. I will close the entrance behind us."

Doug laughed. "It would be a poor Keeper, yadda, yadda, right?"

"Exactly."

"Hold on there, Walker," Cory said. "You can take Danny through whatever that is, if you want to kill him and yourself, but leave me out of it. If that means I have to get out of this chair and wait here so you can push Danny, then I'll do that."

Anger started to boil up in Christy's stomach, but she stopped herself with a breath. She was being selfish, she realized, to both Cory and Abei. "Abei," she said, "where can we go so that we all don't have to continue through these swarms?"

Abei shook his head. "There's no other way. I will lead you."

Christy smiled gratefully. "Then can you help me lift Danny, and help Cory out of the chair?"

"No, Cory needs to go," Brad interrupted.

"Hey, Brad, mind your own business!" Cory yelled.

Christy squeezed Brad's arm for an instant and said soothingly, "Cory's right, Brad. It is dangerous going forward. We could be attacked by those things."

Danny moaned again and leaned over the side of the wheelchair, vomiting.

Abei knelt down and pulled one of Danny's eyelids back. He rose again, shaking his head.

"We may already be too late."

Christy put her hand over her mouth, stifling a cry. "We can't be too late," she said, and reached to touch Danny's brow. "He's not as hot."

Abei shook his head. "He will continue to cool down until he stops breathing."

Christy began pushing the chair, disregarding Cory's protests.

"No, no, no, wait for me!" Brad cried.

"Danny is dying! I can't wait!" Christy screamed.

Brad stepped toward Christy and she thought for a second he was going to attack her, but he grabbed her pack instead and yanked at it.

"Hold on a second!" Christy snapped. She slipped her pack off as Brad pulled at it. He knelt down with the pack and rummaged through it at lightning speed, pulling a small towel out. Then he dug further, flinging the contents out without regard for where anything landed. He found a small bottle of something and emptied it onto the towel, but he moved too fast for Christy to see what it was. Standing up, he bolted ahead, right into the swirling swarms of insects.

"Danny is better," Brad said, waving the towel over his head as he met the first swarm head on. Instead of attacking, the swarm parted, scattering to the non-existent wind.

Christy hastily gathered everything Brad had strewn about and stuffed it back into her pack.

"Thanks, Brad," she said. Grabbing the wheelchair, she followed Brad's path, now clear of the deadly insect mist.

"And this," Utoov said, waving Mike and Doug into a massive chamber decorated with colorful maps and scenes, "is the beginning section of the Empty World's entire history that I mentioned to you." Mike and Doug began to wander at will, gasping at the beautiful scenes that filled every available inch of wall space.

While Mike was examining a particularly vivid section of pictures, rendered in a different style than the surrounding scenes, Utoov came over to him.

"That story was painted by my cousin," Utoov said, almost spitting out the words.

Mike looked at him, and as he explained, his bitterness was evident. "The Ancients used us for their own purposes at all times. My cousin was one of the fortunate among us for a while. He had this talent." Utoov swept his hand past the beautiful scene. "But in the end, it mattered not. He finished his life as a servant to a cruel Ancient."

"What happened? These pictures are wonderful."

Utoov pointed to the small figure of a painted Ancient. "The coat on this figure is not quite the correct shade of blue." Utoov was silent for a moment before continuing. "They did not forgive mistakes of any kind."

Doug walked over to them. "I'd like to see some of those portals you mentioned."

Mike nodded. "Maybe we should take a peek at some of the stored machines first. There may be something we can hitch a ride on."

Doug chuckled and explained himself to Utoov. "Mike and Jack Renfrew found a warehouse of mostly inoperable Ancient machines a while back. A couple still worked and they helped save the day by rescuing me and a boy named Trevor."

Mike grinned. "Pity we had to abandon them."

Utoov shook his head. "Even though you are not Ancients, I can't let you take any machinery from here. It could fall into the Ancients' hands. You are welcome to look though."

Mike shrugged. "Let's see those portals then."

Utoov led the way down a long, brightly lit corridor. He stopped at various spots, pointing out rooms or stairways of interest. He was clearly proud of his charge, despite everything having been invented, constructed, or artistically created by Ancients. He'd been guarding the pyramid for too long to think of it and all of its contents as anything but his.

At one juncture, where corridors diverged in all four directions, Utoov pointed. "Down that way, there are rooms upon rooms of crystals neatly stacked ... not the large crystal I told you about with their whole existence recorded on it, but I imagine the thousands of crystals stored there also cover every bit of knowledge."

"Are you sure they store knowledge and aren't power crystals?" Mike asked.

Utoov considered the question for a second. "I've never checked. Good point."

Gesturing in the opposite direction of the rooms of crystals, Utoov led them to an inconspicuous doorway that slid open the second Utoov stepped in front of it.

"Here we are." Utoov stepped aside to let Mike and Doug enter first.

Doug grabbed Mike's arm as if to steady himself. "I swear the inside is larger than the outside."

Mike was staring up and around, turning his head slowly, taking in the vast space they'd walked into. In one sense, it looked like a stadium filled with levels beyond counting. Each level had rows of arched entryways leading off into the distance. Gleaming metal rails and walkways led up to every level and entryway. Strategically spaced staircases linked each level to its neighbors above and below. A low hum filled the air. Above each entrance was a glowing, spinning, three-dimensional orb.

Utoov explained. "It is larger. I have to give the Ancient's credit. At least those Ancients of thousands of years ago. This whole room is some sort of portal so it's not really even inside the pyramid. That's how the inside is many levels taller than the pyramid outside."

"Unbelievable" Doug mumbled.

"Look!" Mike pointed way up into the distance. The speck above them gradually grew until it resolved into a hovering platform with its own gleaming railing. The platform gently descended, touching down right at their feet. It looked as if it could accommodate three or four people.

"Did you call that?" Doug asked.

"No. It comes automatically once someone steps through the doorway."

"Is there some way of knowing which world can be reached through each archway? Beyond knowing what a particular world looks like, I mean."

Utoov smiled. "I would hope so, because good luck finding Earth. It could take you months if not years to stumble across the spinning globe that is your world. You have no idea how many worlds are represented here, so they made it a bit easier. You need just to step on the platform, speak your destination in any language of your world and you will be brought to that entryway. Inside you will find separate portals to all links within your world."

"So I could come up through my own pond?" Doug asked.

"If your pond is a portal, yes."

"Tempting," Mike said. "But we have to find Jack and the kids first."

Utoov frowned. "You mentioned Jack before. I saw no such human when I found the others."

Mike and Doug looked at each other.

"That's not good news," Doug said. "He must have been separated from the kids somehow."

"Not good news at all," Mike agreed.

"Utoov?" Mike began, thinking aloud. "Are there any portals in that town that the kids were heading to? There must be, right?"

Utoov nodded. "Certainly there used to be. But I also remember that the town was abandoned and the Garlians rebuilt it. It is not the advanced settlement it once was. I am not sure what might still be operational, if anything."

Just then, a muffled bang and then a pattering sound drifted from the corridor they'd come from and filtered into the vast portal room.

"What was that?" Doug asked.

"That," Utoov said as he raced out of the room, "was an explosion. And it came from the pyramid entrance."

On the outskirts of Boakly, stopped next to a hidden entrance to the tunnels under the town, Abei checked Danny again. Once Brad figured out that he could clear the swarms of deadly insects with Christy's insect repellant on a towel, they'd made good time to their destination.

"I will go down by myself and return shortly with the antidote," Abei said.

"Won't that take twice as long? Why can't we go with you?" Christy was looking at Danny. His skin was clammy and getting colder every minute.

"Remember being chased from the tunnels? Do you want to take the chance that the Ancients might still be here and that we could be captured?"

Christy had to shake her head no.

"I will go by myself. Even if the Ancients and the evil Garlians are still below, I will be able to sneak in and procure the antidote without being detected. The little time it would save bringing Danny down with me is not worth the risk."

Abei tripped a hidden mechanism and the entrance opened up. "Brad has one egg remaining. It can't hurt to feed that to Danny. And rub his extremities to restore as much warmth and circulation as possible while I'm gone."

The Garlian waved a grim goodbye and disappeared into the tunnel.

Christy took the last egg from Brad and fed it to Danny.

"Cory, can you rub Danny's right arm and Brad, rub his left arm?"

Cory nodded.

Christy watched for Brad's eyes next. There was just a flicker, but he did make contact. "Thanks, both of you."

Christy stood behind Cory's chair and gingerly took Murray off of his perch on the back of Cory's neck. The cat had been displaced when they'd put Danny on Cory's lap. Since then Murray had been as content as could be expected on his new roost, but now Christy had a job for him to do.

She stepped around in front of the wheelchair and placed Murray on Danny's lap, holding him in place for a second until he was comfortable. "That's it Murray, add your warmth to Danny too."

Christy then knelt down and began rubbing Danny's legs. She kept it up for a few minutes then noticed that Cory was losing interest. "Please, Cory, don't stop."

Cory groaned but continued. "Ok," Christy said, noticing Brad's concentration was also waning, "we're going to sing 'Row, Row, Row Your Boat' while we rub."

Cory glared at Christy but she glared back and began singing, stopping her kneading of Danny's legs just long enough to slap Cory on the side of the head when he didn't immediately join in.

"Ouch!"

"Sing then."

"*Row, row, row your boat, gently down the stream ...*" It was off-key, but at least he was singing. She joined in, smiling.

A few minutes after they started, Brad joined in too, even more off-key than his brother.

CHAPTER 20

"It must be the Ancients who are chasing you. But I can't understand how they used explosives. They do not have explosives," Utoov said as he ran with Mike and Doug back toward the entrance.

Mike interrupted. "Sorry to inform you, but we know that TuMaz-Tan, a particularly nasty Ancient, has found explosives somewhere. He used them to blow up a portal on the coast a while back."

"That is not good. Follow me. If they're able to enter the pyramid, we can only check quickly to see what they're up to. But let's hope the explosion didn't destroy the door."

Within seconds though, Utoov's fears were realized. They heard footsteps and voices and the clanking and scraping of metal as sheathed swords and shouldered spears brushed against walls.

Utoov put up his hands for them to halt. Then he silently motioned them to follow. They bolted up a flight of stairs to a catwalk that ran the length of every corridor in the pyramid.

"We can follow them from up here if we're careful."

Soon they watched as at least three dozen Ancients marched by, grouped tightly together. They were joking and laughing, all except their leader, TuMaz-Tan. Doug tapped Mike as TuMaz passed under their hiding spot. "It had to be that scum," he whispered.

Mike nodded.

They followed the Ancients as they marched up and down corridors until they came to the warehouse of machinery. Mike and Doug hadn't seen that room yet either, and were just as amazed as the Ancients.

TuMaz walked around asking questions of his companions, but they all just kept shaking their heads. None of them knew what they were looking at. Finally, guessing at the meaning of his angry gestures, Mike and Doug figured out that he'd ordered one of the other Ancients to stand guard over the room while the rest of them filed out of the room and then right out of the pyramid altogether.

Utoov beckoned and they followed him quietly to the portal room. Once there, Mike asked Utoov, "What did they say?"

"The boss—"

"TuMaz-Tan," Doug interrupted.

"The boss guy, he was amazed at the warehouse. He kept asking the others what the vehicles and other machines were, but none of them knew anything. I think they finally got frustrated. TuMaz-Tan ordered one of them to guard the room." Utoov fell silent, and he began to sob quietly.

"What's wrong, Utoov?" Doug asked.

"I have failed my charge. The Ancients have discovered the pyramid. All is now lost."

"You'll think of something." Mike said.

"I fear not. Now the Ancients will strip all the knowledge and all the weapons, vehicles, and technology from the pyramid. With that motivated Ancient, TuMaz-Tan, you called him, knowing the extent of what's here, it is as good as all figured out. He will have power beyond belief."

Utoov sat down, sobbing even more.

Mike nudged Doug and the two of them whispered together. After a few minutes, Doug walked over and sat down, putting his hand on Utoov's shoulder.

"Do you think you can find a portal to Boakly? If so, I think we can get closer to the kids. After we find them, I promise to return and help you defend this pyramid from the Ancients."

Mike seconded the offer.

"You'd do that? Both of you?"

"Of course," Doug said, answering for them both. "You are right, Utoov, TuMaz-Tan will figure it all out and use everything in here to his advantage. I have no doubt that his goal is total domination over this world. We can't let that happen. We'll help in any way we can once we find the kids."

Utoov smiled that lipless smile of his. "Then let's go find a working portal, shall we?"

"Where's Abei?" Christy sobbed. "No matter how much we try to keep Danny warm, he's getting colder and colder."

As soon as the words were out of her mouth, a shout came up through the hidden entrance, and seconds later, Abei rushed up holding a small vial in his hands. He was out of breath from running.

"Here, get this into him immediately," he said, handing the vial to Christy.

She wasted no time in gently shaking Danny's head and speaking soothingly to him.

"Danny? You need to take this. Please," she pleaded.

Danny moaned but Christy was able to empty the antidote into his throat and he swallowed it.

"Now we wait," Abei said.

"Were we in time?" Christy asked, wiping her eyes.

Abei shrugged. "We won't know till the antidote gets into his system and starts working ... or doesn't."

They waited. Danny seemed to get neither better nor worse as they watched for signs. Abei kept checking his forehead and looking grim, signaling that he'd sensed no change each time.

Finally he put his hand on Danny's forehead and let out a sigh.

"What?" Christy asked, checking his forehead herself. "He's not hot or cold anymore. Does that mean he's out of danger?"

"Danny's better," Brad said, and they all laughed, finally releasing the tension that had gripped them since Danny had been bitten.

Abei smiled. "Yes Brad, I believe so. Your eggs helped keep him fighting the poison until we could give him the antidote. Without them, we would have been much too late, I fear." Abei paused only briefly before getting back down to business. "Now," he said, "you all need to return with me to the tunnels."

Christy looked at him questioningly.

"The Ancients and their Garlian friends were gone, I had no trouble gathering the antidote. But there is something for you down there," Abei explained. "I will say no more. Come, I'll push the wheelchair through the tunnels till we get to where we're going."

"Where are we going?" Christy asked as they traveled through the tunnels under Boakly.

"Looks like we're headed to the planning room," Cory replied.

Abei smiled and nodded. "Yes, we are."

"Hey, settle down," Cory said half-heartedly as Danny squirmed. He was not yet fully conscious, but showing clear signs of recovery.

They arrived at the entrance to the planning room and Abei held up his hand for silence. It stopped them in their tracks.

"Christy, you first," Abei said. "Brad and I will push Cory's chair."

Christy was about to correct Abei, thinking Brad would ignore the Garlian, but to her surprise, he stepped next to Abei and grabbed the right handle, ready to push.

Smiling, she shrugged and stepped into the planning room.

"Christy!"

"Daddy!"

Running to each other, they met in the middle and clung to one another for a long time.

Mike finally got a chance to hug Christy as explanations and updates were given by all.

By the time their stories had petered out, Danny had his eyes open but still looked as if he was feeling the effects of the flu or, as Doug remarked, a hangover.

"Honey, tell your mom I love her," Doug said, grabbing hold of Christy's hand. "Mike and I are staying. We have to."

"What!"

Utoov called for silence and explained the grave situation the Empty World faced now that the pyramid had been found by TuMaz-Tan.

"This isn't fair. I should stay too," Christy said, frowning.

Doug looked at her with sympathy in his eyes. "Honey, Trevor said that same thing a while back. Remember which side you took?"

"This is different."

Mike shook his head and waved both of his hands as if to brush the thought aside. "This time, young lady, I agree with your dad. All of you kids have to go home."

"We still have to get to a portal," Christy said, almost smugly. "Detective Lockhart, when you came back with Brad and Danny and we split up, my grandpa took the devices that we had and put them in his pack."

She fell quiet thinking of her grandfather and was nearly brought to tears once more. "And now we don't know where he is."

Her dad hugged her again. "Mike and I promise to look for Jack as soon as we can," he said, then shook his head and smiled. "Weren't you listening to our story? Utoov has the lack of devices covered."

Utoov smiled, arms folded across his chest. "Your wish is my command."

Thanks for reading!

You made it to the end! This may be the end of one story, but if you like reading the Empty World Saga, there's more to come. Don't want to miss a release?

Perks of being an Email Insider include:

- Notification of book releases (1-2 times per year)
- Inside track on beta reading
- Access to Inside Exclusive bonus extras and giveaways

Sign up for the my Email Insiders list at:
www.davidkanderson.info

Books by David K. Anderson

Empty World Saga

The first 4 books of the Empty World Saga are available in ebook and paperback.

1. Portal Through the Pond
2. Beyond the Portal
3. At the Portal's End
4. The Lost Portal

Read about the Empty World Saga and discover where to buy at: emptyworldsaga.com

About the Author

Growing up, David K. Anderson was mentored by his Uncle Ralph, a gifted artist who taught him to express himself in creative ways: writing, drawing and sculpting.

David is married and has three adult children. Throughout his adult life, he has volunteered countless hours with children with disabilities involving creative activities. His lifelong passions for art, sculpting and storytelling have helped him combine his talents to create enjoyment for hundreds of children of all abilities. His family's mutual love for fantasy, fiction, and fun along with a desire to ensure that children of all abilities can be heroes, has motivated him to write stories that engage us all.

Made in the USA
Middletown, DE
12 December 2018